The
BARON'S
ROSE

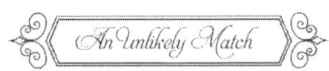
An Unlikely Match

MINDY BURBIDGE STRUNK

ACKNOWLEDGMENTS

Special thanks to my fabulous editor, Jenny Proctor and all my Regency Chicks!

Thanks to my excellent proof reader-Patti Knowlton and my awesome ARC team! This book would be a hot mess without you guys!

Last and most importantly thanks to my family for supporting me and cheering for me. I love you guys more than words can say!

CHAPTER 1

Rose Allen stepped from the carriage, caressing the pearls at
her neck as she looked up at the illuminated yellow stone
façade of Lord Trenton's London town home. Lanterns lit the
walkway and staircase. She pulled her wrap up around her shoulders and tightened it slightly, the chill of spring air only part of the
reason she was cold. Rose closed her eyes. *I can do this. I deserve to
be here.* Her stomach lurched and her cheek twitched. She pushed
the feeling of inadequacy down.

The squeak of the carriage behind her brought Rose's attention
back and she watched as her brother-in-law handed out her sister.
Violet looked up into her husband's face and Rose gritted her teeth
to stop from growling. Watching the two moon over each other
was enough to turn Rose's stomach.

Violet wrapped her hand around her husband's arm and the
two of them preceded Rose up the staircase and into the entryway.
Rose glared at her sister's back. *It should have been me on his arm,
not Violet.*

The butler approached them, and His Grace presented his

1

card. The butler bowed low. "Ah, Your Grace. Welcome to Hawthorne House." He took their wraps, handing them off to a footman standing nearby. "Please, follow Henry. He will lead you to the ballroom."

The duke smiled. "Has my aunt, Lady Mayfield arrived yet?"

The butler gave a slight shake of his head. "No, Your Grace."

The duke's smile faltered slightly, and Rose stood a little taller, a smirk curling her lips. He was new to society. The *ton* would not be kind to him if he were so transparent.

The group trailed after the butler, stopping just outside the ballroom. He motioned them inside.

The duke looked into the ballroom. "I should like to wait a few moments for my aunt to arrive before we enter."

Henry bowed, leaving them to stand in the corridor. The duke took a deep breath and straightened his waistcoat, even as he squared his shoulders.

Rose grinned at his obvious discomfort.

"Well, my love." He spoke quietly to Violet.

Rose bristled at the term of endearment.

"We are not going to get this first encounter over with if we stand here in the corridor." His Adam's apple bobbed a few times before he gave his head a firm nod.

"Can we not wait for your aunt? She was to introduce us."

Rose raised a brow. Must Violet always be such a milquetoast? A duchess needed backbone—something which Violet often lacked.

"She is not here. What are we to do? Stand about looking like a bunch of nodcocks?" Frustration laced the duke's words.

Violet looked up at her husband with worried eyes. "What if they don't like me, Tad? What if I am a complete failure?"

Rose shook her head. The duke had not been raised in England, which meant this was his first entrance into the London

2

social scene. Rose should be the one guiding him through it. After all, she had experienced it before, unlike Violet. Her sister and the duke were like one blind man leading another. Neither of them knew what they were about.

A large part of Rose hoped Violet's fears were realized—that she would be a failure. Perhaps then the duke would understand what a mistake he had made. He should have chosen Rose. Rose had prepared herself for this role. She had done everything she could think of to become a duchess. Rose's cheek twitched. It had been for naught. Violet had convinced the duke that she was the one he loved, not Rose.

The duke put his free hand on top of the hand Violet had wrapped around the crook of his arm. From the way his muscles flexed, Rose guessed he was giving Violet a reassuring squeeze. "It's not possible. No one could ever find you lacking." He smiled at her and Rose's hands clenched at her side.

"Well, prattling on out here in the hall is achieving nothing. Can we not continue on inside?" Rose asked, before letting out a deep sigh, her eyes narrowing slightly.

Violet flinched at the harshness of Rose's voice, but Rose brushed her sister's response aside. It was just another example of Violet's timidity.

The duke led his wife into the ballroom; Rose walked several steps behind. She looked up at the large chandelier, sparkling with thousands of crystals, hundreds of candle flames reflecting off the cut glass.

She swallowed hard. This was everything she remembered from her first and only Season. Ladies and gentlemen dotted the room, all dressed in the finest fabrics. Rose sucked in a deep breath. *This time it will be different.* This time she would come away with an offer—she had to. This was her last chance. At one and twenty, her time was running out.

"It's enchanting," Violet murmured over her shoulder. "Do you not think so, Tad?"

Rose moved forward a few steps, bringing her even with Violet and the duke.

He looked down on his wife and smiled. "If you are happy, my love, then I am happy."

Rose grunted and took several steps to the side, distancing herself from their irritating felicity.

"Stop gawking like a couple of ninnies' and let's present you to our hosts," Lady Mayfield said, bustling toward them, her niece Miss Standish, fallowing behind.

"Really, nephew," the older woman whispered when she neared. "Do you wish everyone to think you were raised a common shopkeeper? Did we not review this just yesterday?"

The duke breathed in deeply, his shoulders raising and falling. He ran his hand along the back of his neck and narrowed his gaze at his aunt. "Perhaps if you had been on time, I should not have had to wait about, looking like a commoner."

Lady Mayfield guffawed. "I arrived on time. *You* arrived early." She shook her head, her jowls swinging back and forth.

"What is their name again?" The duke whispered as he straightened to his full height, his face setting in a stony look of aloofness.

Lady Mayfield let out an exasperated sigh. "Lord and Lady Trenton."

Violet, like her husband, straightened her back, and lifted her chin regally as they neared the start of the receiving line.

Lord Trenton smiled and nodded to everyone he greeted. His wife, however, was a complete contrast. Few of the guests received even the slightest upturn of her lips. Most only earned a frown, or in a few cases, an outright scowl.

As she neared their host, Rose took a deep, calming breath.

This was where it started. This ball would help define her Season and she was not going to ruin it. She pasted a brilliant smile on her lips and gave her cheeks a discreet pinch.

Lady Mayfield approached Lord Trenton. "My Lord, may I introduce my nephew, His Grace, the Duke of Shearsby."

"Ah, Your Grace. I have been most anxious to make your acquaintance." Lord Trenton quite literally bounced with excitement, as he simultaneously bowed and shook the duke's hand. He then turned his eyes onto Violet.

Lady Mayfield followed his gaze. "And his new wife, Her Grace, the Duchess of Shearsby." Lady Mayfield nodded in Rose's direction. "Miss Rose Allen and my niece, Miss Jessica Standish."

Lord Trenton smiled widely at them and Rose felt her breath slowly drain from her lungs. She clasped her trembling hands tightly in front of her. Dare she hope that society wouldn't shun her after all?

Lady Trenton turned narrowed eyes on them. "You brought the sister? I don't recall including her in the invitation."

Rose's smile dropped into a sort of grimace, her hope evaporating and her earlier fears pressing down heavily on her shoulders.

Lady Mayfield harrumphed. "An oversight on your part, I am sure."

A fuzzy ringing filled Rose's ears as she watched the two ladies stare at each other, both leaning in, daring the other to step back and lose the nonverbal argument. The music sounded far away, drowned out by four words, repeating over and over in Rose's mind.

You brought the sister.

Rose's cheeks flamed and a burning sensation filled her eyes.

Finally, after several long moments of awkward silence, Lady Trenton leaned back on her heels, giving the win to Lady

Mayfield. In any other moment, Rose would have shared in the win, but tonight she could not.

"You are holding up the line, Lady Mayfield." Lady Trenton flicked her wrists, motioning them away from her. "Please, find someone else you can impose upon."

Lady Mayfield lifted her nose, glaring down at their hostess. "Lady Trenton. Still a bit high in the instep, I see." She turned on her heel and moved toward the throng of people already occupying the ballroom.

Rose allowed herself to be pulled along by Miss Standish, who at some point had put her hand at Rose's elbow.

"Pay her no mind, Miss Allen. My aunt Mayfield says Lady Trenton thinks herself the tops of the trees, but it is only a charade because her husband has wandering eyes." Miss Standish smiled kindly, which only served to intensify the burning in Rose's eyes. The girl was young and knew nothing of society. If she pitied Rose, things must be dire, indeed.

The little group found chairs opposite the terrace doors. Rose looked longingly at those doors. If she could go out to the terrace, perhaps she could disappear into the night and be done with it all. Living as a spinster or even a governess could not be so bad as this.

"Violet, may I claim you for the next set?" The duke smiled down at his wife. Violet looked over at Rose with the same pitying gaze Miss Standish wore. The duke also glanced over. It was more than Rose could take.

"I am in need of air. Please, excuse me." Rose pushed herself to standing, wanting to run until she reached the doors or beyond.

Miss Standish stood also. "Would you like some company, Miss Allen?"

"No!" Several people turned at Rose's shout. She lowered her voice, trying not to give the guests around them anything more to gossip about. "No, thank you. I will return shortly."

Miss Standish's brow furrowed, but she sat back down in her chair.

Violet placed a hand on Rose's arm, her expression asking if Rose wanted her to come. Rose shook it off. Violet was the last person Rose wished to have join her on the terrace. In point of fact, she was the last person Rose wanted to return home with at the end of this dreadful evening. She wanted, no, *needed* to be alone with her thoughts, if only for a moment.

Rose skirted the room as quickly as was proper. Barely halfway to her destination, she passed behind a group of ladies, most of whom she knew from her last Season.

"I should wonder at her thinking she would be welcome among polite society after being thrown over so completely." Miss Partridge leaned forward slightly, obviously desiring all the ladies to hear her disparaging words.

Rose slowed her steps, unable to keep herself from listening. Of whom were they speaking? She looked around the ballroom, looking for someone whose Season seemed as dire as her own.

"And by her own sister, no less. I should not show my face in society, let alone Town, again." Miss Pulley sat back, her arms folded daintily in her lap.

"Well I should think it served Miss Allen right."

Rose sucked in a breath, freezing in her tracks.

"She thought herself so far above us, dismissing us so rudely upon our last meeting." The anger in Miss Carlyle's voice was unmistakable. "Oh, look. Mr. Fairchild is walking this way. I have noticed him watching me for some time."

Miss Pulley scoffed. "I believe you are mistaken. It is I he has been staring at."

Not wanting to be caught listening to their conversation, Rose rushed the rest of the way to the terrace doors. As she exited the crowded ballroom, the cool evening air crashed against her overheated body. She moved to the farthest edge of the cobblestone veranda, finding a slightly darkened corner to retreat into. She placed her elbows on the rock wall separating it from the garden beyond, and dropped her head into her hands, scrubbing at her brow with her fingers.

Her Season was ended before it had even begun. In her mind, she had known the possibility of it being a success had been scarce, but to watch the reality of it crash down before her eyes was worse than she had imagined. She looked around for a moment and contemplated fleeing the ball entirely. But she knew such an action would only give the gossips more to find lacking in her character.

She should not have come. But now that she had, she would be expected to smile and submit to the smug looks and overtly cruel comments which the ton would undoubtedly bestow upon her. Rose pressed her lips together, pushing her shoulders back. She could do this. She could show everyone she did not care for their opinion. All she need do was get through this evening. Then, if she so desired, she could withdraw from society.

Rose inhaled through her nose, letting the air push through her lips on the way out. She moved back toward the nearest set of open doors. Pausing, she closed her eyes and took one last calming breath, before she stepped back inside the ballroom.

"Oh, there you are Miss Allen. I have come to fetch you." Lady Mayfield grabbed her by the arm and propelled her toward a group of gentlemen gathered by another set of doors. Rose recognized Lord Timothy, Mr. Penderton and Lord Kent, but the other gentlemen were unknown to her.

Lady Mayfield thrust her in front of a tall gentleman. He was not wholly unappealing, but he was also not what Rose would consider handsome. "Lord Munsford. I should like to introduce you to Miss Rose Allen." She gave Rose a little shove forward. "Miss Allen, Lord Munsford."

Lord Munsford and his broad shoulders bowed. "I am pleased to make your acquaintance. May I have the next set, Miss Allen?"

Lord Kent and several of the men next to him laughed behind their gloved hands. Rose glanced between them and Lord Munsford, who stood directly in front of her. Was he asking her as a joke for his friends to laugh over later?

She narrowed her eyes at him. His lips did not quiver, his shoulders did not shake. Either he was very good at role playing or he was sincere in his offer. Rose could not tell which. If she should refuse him, she would most certainly be done dancing for the evening. But if she were merely the object of teasing, could she bear it for the entirety of the set?

Rose nodded her head. Whether she was the joke or not, she could not afford to reject any gentleman. Even one whose hair stuck out in every which direction.

Lady Mayfield patted Rose on the arm. "It appears my use is done here. I shall return to my seat with the other matrons." Lady Mayfield shuffled away, leaving Rose to stare after her. Was this the lady's way of being kind? Or was she merely setting Rose up for more embarrassment, as a way of getting even for what Rose had done to Violet and the duke?

"This way, Miss Allen." Lord Munsford led her to the dance floor, her mind still trying to figure out if this arrangement was for her good or her detriment.

CHAPTER 2

Oliver entered the dimly lit morning room of Brooks's, assessing the room and its occupants. He walked to the farthest corner and found a quiet spot next to a window. With the exception of the billiards room, this was his favorite spot. Oliver sat down and opened the morning newspaper, blocking out everything surrounding him. His taut muscles made his whole body stiff. He had just finished meeting with Mr. Beaverton, his father's solicitor. Every time he met with Beaverton, the extent of his late father's debt increased. Each blow came as a complete surprise to Oliver, although his mother did not seem nearly so shocked.

Oliver ran a hand through his hair, a sigh coming out as more of a groan. What was he to do? He was now responsible for his mother and sister *and* a large estate, but with no inheritance to assist him.

"That was a heavy sigh, indeed. Have you also escaped for some peace and quiet?"

Oliver grunted low in his throat and straightened his paper, raising it a little higher in hopes it would deter any further conversation.

"I simply could not stand another minute. It's unconscionable, a man being driven out of his own home." The man gave a slight huff. "One of us had to leave and seeing as she seemed in no hurry to depart, it fell to me."

Oliver closed his eyes. Apparently, this interloper was not well versed in the social etiquette of a gentlemen's club. Did he not understand the newspaper was simply a barrier—a signal indicating conversation was not welcome? Sooner or later the man must take the hint and leave. Surely, he would not continue to prattle on, especially if there was no response to his questions.

Oliver was in no mood for idle chitchat. His club was the only place he found solitude. It was one of the many reasons Oliver had originally chosen Brooks's over White's, which was the club his father had frequented. Thomas Brandon would never have lowered himself to mingle with the Whig riffraff polluting the halls of Brooks's and so it was the perfect club for Oliver. He was not about to let this gentleman rob him of his solitude.

Oliver discreetly looked around the side of his paper. The gentleman sat, looking out the window, his hands on his thighs, his legs bouncing restlessly. The gentleman flicked his gaze back, forcing Oliver to return his eyes to the paper. Perhaps this gentleman just needed a little acknowledgment and then he could be on his way. "If your objections to the lady are so strong, perhaps you should not have married her." Oliver did not so much as lower the paper a fraction of an inch.

"Oh, you misunderstand. It is not my wife which brought me here. I could spend months at a time in her company. It is her sister I was speaking of."

Oliver made no more comment, hoping the story was at an end.

"She is come to town with us; my wife is sponsoring her for another season. It was more than her father could manage this year." Looking at him from around his paper, Oliver saw the man run a hand down his thigh, a slow breath hissing through his lips. "My apologies. You are obviously here for some solitude and I am giving you anything but. I will leave you to your paper." The man put his hands on the arms of his chair and began to lift himself to standing.

A tinge of guilt twisted in Oliver's stomach and he lowered his barrier, folding up the paper and placing it in his lap. He looked at the man, his mouth turning up slightly. He recognized the Duke of Shearsby from the Trenton's ball a few nights past. "No. Please do not go on my account, Your Grace. You are correct, I was escaping. But it does not follow that your interruption is unwelcome."

The duke's face colored slightly. "You find me at a disadvantage. For you know me, but I do not believe we have been introduced."

Oliver stood and presented his hand to the duke. "Oliver Brandon, Lord Munsford. We were not officially introduced at Lord Trenton's ball, but I was fortunate enough to dance with Miss Allen." Oliver cleared his throat. "She was, indeed, charming."

She wasn't charming. Beautiful, yes, but certainly not charming. The lady had looked on him with narrowed eyes and suspicion for the entirety of the set they had danced together. In truth, he could likely place the blame on his idiot friends, who had found it immensely amusing that Oliver had been tricked into asking Miss Allen to dance in the first place. Lady Mayfield, it seemed, was doing her best to help repair the girl's reputation; an unlikely goal, even for the likes of Lady Mayfield, from what Oliver had heard.

A servant approached with a tray, cutting short the introduction. He bowed deeply. "As you requested, Your Grace."

The duke smiled with a nod. "Thank you, Simmons."

The servant gave another bow and hurried away.

"Would you care to join me?" The duke inclined his head toward the tray resting on the low table between them.

"I would, thank you." Oliver studied him closer as he poured out two cups of...chocolate? The gabsters had been speculating about this new duke since the death of the old one, nearly two years previous. Rumor said he had been living abroad—India or the West Indies or some such place—before the family solicitor had located him.

Even Oliver's father had gotten in on the gossip about the man, practically insisting Oliver develop a friendship with him, if ever the event arose. His father must be smiling down on the interaction, even now.

"Few people would call Miss Allen charming." The duke looked at Oliver with appraising eyes. "My wife was impressed with the flowers you sent to the house yesterday. She thought them quite lovely."

"And what of Miss Allen? Did she also find them to her liking?" Oliver picked up his cup, the chocolate wafting to his nose. He stared down into the cup, his brow furrowed. He had tasted chocolate on a few occasions and found it lacking.

"If you add a touch of cream and sugar, it is much better. My mother prefers it bitter, but not me." The duke scooted the cream and sugar toward Oliver.

He did as the duke suggested, stirring the hot liquid. "Did not all the gentlemen she danced with send a token?"

"All the gentlemen who danced with her *did* send flowers." The duke grimaced and colored slightly. "I am afraid my sister-in-law's first ball of the Season did not prove to be the success she had hoped."

This man did not act like a duke. He had an easy smile, but

there was also a hint of anxiety or unease about him. Maybe it was the way he picked at invisible lint on the arms of his jacket.

The duke threw back the rest of his chocolate and poured more into his cup, before sitting back in his chair. Oliver squinted at the duke as an air of power emanated from him. Had Oliver really seen uncertainty only moments before? Perhaps he had been wrong, for the man before him now showed no signs of weakness.

"No? I am surprised a lady as lovely as Miss Allen would not be more in demand." Oliver's voice hitched slightly, a trait which had always indicated he was lying. He chided himself inwardly, though the duke didn't know him well enough to recognize the tell. Oliver put his cup back on the tray and sat back, folding his arms across his chest.

The duke raised his brows. "I find that difficult to believe. I am not a dolt, Lord Munsford, nor am I deaf. I heard the gossip people bandied about regarding Miss Allen. I should not think you ignorant of it."

Oliver grimaced at the duke's frankness. "I confess, I have heard things as well. But I make it a habit not to give credence to rumors."

The duke placed his elbows on the arms of the chair, steepling his fingers in front of his chin. "Then you know what she is up against, and at no fault of her own. I fear she will end up a spinster, unless I can do something to prevent it."

"What is to be done?" Oliver knew there would be few options for a lady in Miss Allen's position. "Is this why you have come to Brooks's?"

The duke's head rolled around on his shoulders as if he could not decide whether to nod or shake it. "She is unhappy with my wife and me. She blusters about the house, huffing and scowling but without saying a word." He shook his head. "You can feel her when she enters a room. And so here I am, hiding out like a coward at my club."

Oliver nodded, understanding the need to escape family and the complications that accompany them.

"When we arrived in London, I had hopes that her situation would not be as bad as my aunt had predicted, but after Lord Trenton's ball, I am afraid Lady Mayfield was right. I now believe the only chance she has of making any sort of match will require a substantial increase in her dowry, which will only bring out the worst sort of fortune hunters—a fate I should not wish upon even Miss Allen."

Oliver looked into his cup, swirling the last few sips around the bottom. The man was right. Miss Allen was beyond redemption in the eyes of the *ton*. A large dowry would be the only thing to entice a man to be leg shackled to such a lady. "How much is the lady's dowry now?" Not that Oliver could be enticed, even with the troubles he was facing. He was not *that* sort of a gentleman.

"Seven thousand. But I have been thinking on raising it to ten."

Oliver felt his mouth drop open. Seven thousand pounds was a substantial amount, but ten? Ten thousand could go a long way in saving his family from the financial ruin his father had left to them. Oliver licked his lips, trying to regain his composure. He did not want to be that sort of gentleman, but ten thousand pounds?

"You are correct. Such an amount would subject her to the worst kinds of men." Oliver's stomach churned. Could he become such a man?

The duke looked at him, his eyes narrowing. "What I need is to find a man *for* her, before the fortune hunters come calling." The duke leaned forward. "My aunt tells me you may be just the kind of man I am looking for."

Oliver swallowed the chocolate in his mouth, nearly choking. He set the cup down and sat back in his seat. Was the duke suggesting an arrangement between Oliver and Miss Allen? "I don't know what to say, Your Grace."

The duke leveled a stare at Oliver, one that made him want to crawl beneath his seat. "I thought I was obvious, Lord Munsford. I wish to arrange a marriage between Miss Allen and you."

Now Oliver was the one picking invisible lint off of his coat sleeves. The offer was tempting—more than tempting. Could he really jump headlong into an agreement with a woman he barely knew, when what he *did* know of her was not something to recommend her?

But then, in his present circumstances, could he afford *not* to accept? Such a decision was not to be made quickly or without thought. Turning down the Duke of Shearsby could hold severe repercussions of its own.

Oliver's stomach turned again. His family's financial troubles, were not, as yet, common knowledge, but it would only be a matter of time before all the *ton* knew of the debt his father had left behind. Once the *ton* learned of it, Oliver's prospects would be significantly limited. He leaned forward, placing his elbows on his knees, his chin in his hands. The duke may not even wish to continue discussions once he learned how dire things truly were.

Oliver swallowed hard. "Before you make such an agreement, I think you should be made aware of my family's financial difficulties. My father made some poor investments before his death, leaving my family in an unfortunate situation. In truth, if I agree, I should be no different than the fortune hunters we discussed earlier, because I would be marrying her for her dowry."

The duke now leaned forward, moving his elbows to his knees, but keeping his steepled fingers on his chin. Less than two hands separated the two men's noses. "I believe your honesty makes you very different from the men I described earlier. I understand that any man who agrees to marry Miss Allen will be doing it for the money. But that does not follow that you are a cruel man who will treat her ill, nor a spendthrift who will leave her with nothing and then move on to another." The duke looked intensely at Oliver. "My aunt says you are a good man and I am wont to believe her."

Oliver returned the duke's gaze. "May I have some time to think on it before I give you my decision?"

The duke nodded. "I can only afford a few days. I must have your answer by tomorrow, next. You understand, if you should decide against it, I shall need time to discover my other options."

Oliver nodded. "I understand."

The duke stood up and Oliver followed suit. "I believe we shall become good friends, Lord Munsford. Regardless of your decision about Miss Allen." He inclined his head slightly and moved out from behind the low table sitting between them. "I shall await your answer."

Oliver watched him disappear through the doorway, a new weight settling on his shoulders. If he could only keep someone else from sitting across from him, he may be able to think through this new wrinkle. He sighed. Who was he kidding? This was more than a wrinkle. It was a full-on rip.

CHAPTER 3

G ray clouds drifted across the sky, covering the sun and casting the gardens below in a dark shadow. Rose dropped her head to the windowpane. Gray—it was exactly how she felt today. And yesterday. And the four months before that. She ran a finger down the pane. Why did she keep lying to herself? She did not feel gray—she felt black inside. At times the darkness felt so thick, she thought it might suffocate her.

Even if she did manage to secure a match, it could never be for love. How could anyone love a soul as black as hers?

Rose glanced at the small bouquet of flowers sitting on her dressing table. The arrangement was not lavish, containing only a few sprigs of bluebells and a yellow rose, telling much about the sender. He either held her in little regard or was lacking in funds. Rose feared it may, in fact, be both.

She released a stuttering breath, trying not to let the despair which had begun at Lord Trenton's ball to totally consume her. It was not an easy task, especially when she was alone in her chambers. Her mind drifted of its own accord to that dreadful night and the horrible things she had heard spoken about herself. The worst of it was she knew the things she'd heard were true, though not in the way society believed. It was actually so much worse. Violet and the duke had kept the worst part of the story quiet. Rose told herself they owed her that much, but deep down, when she was truly alone with her thoughts, she knew they owed her nothing.

To add salt to her wounds, Lord Munsford had been the only gentleman to ask her to dance, and that was only at the coaxing of Lady Mayfield. Rose had heard the ladies in the retiring room after the set finished, commenting that Rose had been engaged to a duke and now she could only get a baron of modest means to ask her for a dance.

She swallowed painfully past the lump in her throat, watching as the wind picked up and swirled the dirt on the cobblestone path in the garden.

I must do something, or I shall go mad. Rose pushed herself off the window seat. A turn about the gardens seemed out of the question, but the duke's townhouse was large enough she might squander away some of her time just wandering the corridors.

She left her room and descended to the second floor. The gallery seemed as good a place as any to hide from Violet and still be entertained. The dukes and earls from centuries past looked a good deal more miserable than Rose. It was comforting to know she was not the only one.

The corridor to the gallery would take her past the duke's study, but he rarely kept his door open, which meant Rose could pass by without having to see him. Why she had agreed to let Violet and the duke sponsor her for another season was beyond her. A moment of guilt was all she could owe to it.

As Rose neared the door to the duke's study, she noticed it was cracked open. Rose paused, ready to turn and retreat before either the duke or Violet could see her and engage her in conversation. But the sound of her name stopped her in her tracks.

"What do you mean, you have taken care of the Rose situation, Tad?" Violet's voice carried through the small opening in the doorway.

"I have spoken with several gentleman and I believe I have come to an agreement with one. He asked for a chance to think on my offer, but I believe in the end he will agree." The duke must have moved closer to the window because his voice lowered at the end.

"To what offer will he be agreeing?"

Rose tiptoed closer to the door in order to catch Violet's quieting voice.

The duke turned around, facing the doorway and Rose stepped to the side, pressing her back against the wall.

"To marry Rose, of course. What other arrangements should I make concerning her?"

"Just how many gentlemen have you approached? Have we not done enough damage to her reputation? Must you make her appear desperate?"

Rose leaned forward, peering into the room, twisting the curl at the side of her face around her finger. Not only had the duke thrown her over, but now he was dangling her about to anyone willing to take her off his hands.

"Well," he hedged, "she is desperate. You were at the Trenton's ball. You heard what was said of her." He rubbed a hand across the back of his neck, obviously uncomfortable with the tension between he and his wife. "Besides, I should not say I made an offer to the first three. It was more testing to see if they would be inclined to such a thing."

Violet's hands went to her face as her head shook slightly. It was the first time Rose had seen anything remotely close to a disagreement between her sister and the duke. It almost sounded as if Violet was defending Rose to the duke—standing up for her.

The duke stepped over and stood in front of Violet. "I did not actually make them an offer and I did not use your sister's name. I was only making inquiries; it should not disparage her reputation any."

Violet removed her hands from her face but continued to shake her head. "Just as choosing me did not? You need not have come right out with it, Tad. I am certain, unless the men were completely bacon brained, they knew exactly whom and what you were speaking about."

"All that is irrelevant." The duke waved away Violet's argument. "I found someone else and I believe he will accept my terms." He paused. "I did need to add another three thousand pounds to her dowry, but—"

"Three thousand pounds?" Rose heard her own voice shriek from the corridor. "You had to offer me up for ten thousand pounds and the gentleman still had to think about it?" Could things get any worse? There was a time she would have been flattered to have such a dowry. But now, was she truly such a blight that ten thousand pounds could not complete the deal?

The duke and Violet's eyes swung toward the doorway, both looking equally guilty and contrite.

"And who is this pillar of the ton which is considering your generous offer?" Rose spat out.

Violet stepped in front of her husband, as if she were protecting him from Rose. As if such an action was needed. Rose narrowed her eyes at them, her hands balling at her sides. Perhaps Violet knew what she was about after all.

"Lord Munsford." The duke straightened his back and raised a brow, giving her one of his duke looks. Well, Rose would not be cowed.

"Lord Munsford? You could not even foist me off on someone better than a pockets to let baron?"

The duke stepped out from behind his wife and walked to the fireplace, grabbing a book resting on the mantle. "You get your precious title, Rose. You will be Lady Munsford. Considering the circumstances, I should think any title would be welcome."

"A baron? Am I to thank you for arranging for me to marry a baron?" Her gaze swung over to Violet. "I was to be a duchess, not merely a baroness." She nearly spit the words out.

Violet stepped forward. "Our mother was a baroness. Are you so much better than she, Rose?"

"Don't bring Mama into this, Violet. You know that was not my intent."

Violet looked at Rose, sadness evident in her eyes, then turned away. She wrapped her arms around her middle and stared out the windows. "I cannot take it back, Rose. I cannot undo what has been done. But we *are* trying to help."

"If you could take it back—and let me have him—would you?" Rose knew the answer, but she wanted to hear her sister say it out loud.

"No. I would not."

"Then do not act as though you are remorseful," Rose sneered.

Violet turned around. "What of you, Rose? Would you take it back if you could? Would you take back luring me to the orangery so Mr. McPhail could take me at knife point and force me to marry him?"

Rose took a step back.

"Just as I thought. Do not speak to me of true remorse until you are ready to take responsibility for your part in the matter." Violet straightened her back and raised her chin. "What, Rose? Did you not expect such an outburst from a milquetoast?"

What had happened to her sister? Violet had rarely spoken to anyone in such a manner.

The duke walked over to his wife and pulled her into an embrace.

Rose looked away. She had never felt anything but mild interest in the duke while they were engaged; watching him interact with Violet, seeing the obvious love he had for her made Rose's chest ache. She had never thought she wanted a love match. She had not seen many of them in her lifetime. Rose knew her mother and father had loved one another, but her mother had died so long ago, she had not been old enough to understand what her parents had. Violet and the duke were the first people Rose had seen in love. And while she doubted Violet's sincerity, the duke's was undeniable.

Channeling all her righteous anger, she turned on the duke, her teeth clenched, her hands shaking at her side. "You forgot something in your scheme to be rid of me, Your Grace. And that is that I am not likely to accept Lord Munsford, should he offer for me. I should sooner apply to be a governess than be sold off to anyone who will take me." Her voice hitched on the last words, but she didn't care.

Not willing to hear the duke's reply, she turned on her heel and walked from the room. As she turned down the corridor, she ran head long into Mr. Dawson, the duke's closest friend and secretary.

"Move out of my way, sir." Rose shoved him away and walked quickly down the remainder of the corridor. She ran when she reached the staircase, taking the steps two at a time. When she reached her room, she slammed the door shut and threw herself on her bed.

Her eyes burned and her throat contracted painfully, but no tears came. It seemed there was humiliation so great it was beyond her natural reactions. A governess? Rose laugh-cried. As if she would stoop to such actions. But it would be good to let Violet and the duke think on it for a spell.

Rose pounded her fist and screamed into her pillow. Who did the duke think he was? She was not some colt he could sell off at his leisure. She rolled over onto her back and stared up at the ceiling. Except, she was precisely that. Since her father was obviously not able to be bothered with her, the lot had fallen to Violet and His Grace. The duke was acting like a duke and like her guardian.

Rose rubbed at her forehead with her thumb and forefinger.

A knock sounded on her door.

Rose remained quiet. She knew it was Violet come to make peace. That is what Violet did. She ruined everything and then sought reconciliation. Well, Rose wanted nothing to do with it. Violet was only coming to sooth her conscience, that was all.

"Rose. I know you are in there. Please, may I come in?"

Rose rolled to her side, placing her back to the door.

She heard a slight creak as Violet shifted on her feet. Most would think she had turned to leave, but Rose knew better. This was not the first time Violet had come seeking absolution. Not even the first time this week. Well, Rose would not be the one to give it to her. Violet had betrayed her in the cruelest way, and she deserved to suffer.

Rose's cheek twitched and she lifted a hand to rub at it.

"Rose. I know you are angry with me...with both of us. I only wish we could talk about it. I hate that you will not speak to me. We were so close when we were girls. What happened?"

Mama and Papa loved you best. That is what happened. Rose pulled a pillow over and put it over her head. She didn't want to listen to Violet's sorrowful voice through the door.

"Go away, Violet. I don't want to talk," she whispered into the pillow. There was no way Violet had heard her, but perhaps she had sensed the finality of Rose's silence. A sigh sounded through the door. "When you are ready to talk, you know where I will be."

Rose threw the pillow off of her head, hearing Violet's soft footsteps retreating down the corridor.

When the steps disappeared, Rose quietly got up and cracked the door open, peering down the empty corridor. A moment later, harp music drifted to Rose's ears.

Rose dropped her head against the door frame. How could they sell her off for ten thousand pounds? She slumped farther. *What if ten thousand wasn't enough?*

CHAPTER 4

Oliver rolled the brim of his hat along his thigh, his eyes roving around the parlor of the duke's townhouse. The room was richly furnished—grander than Oliver's family townhouse had been before he'd had to sell off most of the more expensive pieces.

The comparison reminded him of why he was there—what he was about to do. It was not his first choice. It wasn't even his ninth or tenth choice. But it was his only choice.

His father had relegated him to the role of fortune hunter. The phrase turned over in Oliver's mind and his stomach. He had heard it from the lips of more than one lady the evening before at Mrs. Worthington's card party. It seemed all of the *ton* was aware of his father's folly.

The door opened and the duke strode purposefully into the room.

Oliver stood and offered a slight bow. The duke dipped his head and nodded toward the chair across the desk from where he settled.

"Ah, Lord Munsford. I was beginning to wonder if I had sent you scurrying back to the country."

Oliver instinctively sat up taller. He knew this man could destroy him and his family, but nevertheless, Oliver did not want to show weakness. Something told him it would only make the duke dislike him.

Oliver took a discreet shallow breath to calm his racing heart. This was it.

"Of course not, Your Grace. I only needed time to think through your generous offer. It was not something to take lightly."

The duke nodded, leaning forward slightly in his seat. He placed his elbows on the desk, dropping his chin onto his clasped fingers. He raised a brow. "And what have you decided?"

Oliver placed his hat on his crossed knee. "I have decided to accept your offer. I believe few men could refuse it."

The duke nodded and gave a wry grin. "That was the general idea." He sat back in his seat and folded his arms across his chest. "There are some provisions I must insist upon before we call the deal done. But I think we can begin the process."

Oliver nodded. Provisions? What kind of provisions? Oliver felt his neck muscles tense. He should have known there would be conditions to the agreement. Ten thousand pounds was a great deal of money, even for someone with Miss Allen's tainted reputation. "What did you have in mind?"

The duke leaned to the side, resting his elbow on the chair's arm. His other arm rested on the desktop, his fingers flipping a penknife around in a circle.

Oliver watched the sharp blade spin.

"While Miss Allen may disagree, I am not engaging in this arrangement to be rid of her. I should not mind, in the least, supporting her for the remainder of her life, but such things would not make her happy." He stopped flipping the knife and looked at

Oliver. "I must make sure she is protected, personally and financially."

Oliver licked his lips. Where was the duke going with this?

"You already disclosed that you were in some financial difficultly. I have taken the liberty of inquiring more extensively after your circumstances."

Oliver opened his mouth to speak, but the duke raised his hand and a brow.

"I am giving over my sister-in-law and ten thousand pounds, my lord. I would be a fool to do so without some idea of what you are about."

Oliver's shoulders dropped. Nothing good could come from the direction this conversation was taking.

"I was pleased to discover your current financial situation was none of your doing. Your father seems to be the culprit, is he not? From what I discovered, you do not gamble, nor participate in ventures of questionable origin. You are respectable in every way. What's more, your father doesn't seem to be the blackguard, but rather a victim of his own poor judgment."

Oliver looked questioningly at the duke. This was not what he had expected. His shoulders relaxed slightly. "What does this mean for the arrangement?"

"It means I will allow the arrangement to move forward. However, I'll not allow Miss Allen's dowry to be used toward ventures which I deem questionable. It will be written into our agreement that I or Miss Allen must be consulted before her dowry is used."

Oliver's mouth dropped open. This was most uncommon and rather demeaning. "Then you are to hold the purse strings? I should wonder why, when you just stated I was a respectable man in every way." He would be the mockery of the *ton*. No one would take him seriously when they learned he had to ask permission of his wife or even worse, the duke, whenever he had need to use the funds. Which, given their financial situation, would be immediately. What had he gotten himself into? If he should back out now, he would very likely earn the ire, and in all likelihood, an enemy of the duke. But if he accepted the terms, he would appear weak and desperate.

Oliver stared at the duke. He *was* desperate. This was his only way out of his current predicament. Still, there had to be a way to keep some of his dignity, even if it was only a very little amount.

"I am sorry, but I cannot agree to those terms." Oliver swallowed as the duke looked at him with narrowed eyes.

"You have come here to waste my time then?"

Oliver shook his head. "No. Not at all. But I believe, once married, our finances should be between Miss Allen and myself. She seems a capable woman. I don't believe she needs your help in deciding how her money is to be spent."

The duke studied him for a long moment. "You will consult with Miss Allen before spending her dowry. Can you agree with that?

Oliver nodded.

"Then I believe we have an agreement." The duke's mouth turned up slightly. "There is the small matter of Miss Allen accepting your offer of marriage. She is..." He looked to the ceiling. "She is not currently inclined to accept such an offer."

What? The lady was *not inclined* to accept such an offer? Why go through this ruse, if she was not wont to accept? "*An* offer or *my* offer?" Was it him or marriage in general?

Did it matter? Yes, it did matter to him. He wanted a wife who at least respected him, even if she felt unhappy with the circumstances of the marriage.

The duke shrugged. "Miss Allen has had several disappointments in recent months. She is a bit...disheartened at the moment."

He leaned forward in his chair and waved a hand in front of him. "But I am convinced I can prevail upon her to accept. I believe a special license will be helpful in that regard."

It was Oliver's turn to lean forward. "A special license?" The words stuck in his throat. "I couldn't possibly—" The money was only part of the issue. Oliver did not think he could get an audience with the Archbishop, even if he did have the money. Before his father's ill-conceived investments, Oliver's family had not been considered wealthy. Comfortable, with a sizable estate and title, was the best they could boast. Oliver's shoulders tightened again, the weight of what he was consenting to settling squarely on his back. In all of his musing about this decision, Oliver had never thought about the effect being related to a duke would have upon his life. Oliver would be expected to associate—and everything that entailed—with people far outside his normal social circle. He knew of these people and would be voting alongside them in Parliament, but he did not typically engage in tea with dukes.

The duke waved Oliver aside as he stood. "I can help with that, not to worry." Oliver quickly stood up. The duke walked around the desk and clapped Oliver on the shoulder. "Come. Let us go find the ladies." He took a deep breath. "May as well get this over with." Oliver almost did not hear him, so quietly he muttered as the two walked toward the door.

Oliver paused, but hurried to catch up when the duke did not. "Perhaps we should not bother them today, Your Grace."

This time the duke paused. "Please, call me Shearsby."

Oliver smiled at the intimacy the name implied.

"If you think delaying this will make it better," Shearsby replied "you are mistaken. In point of fact, I believe it will only make it worse."

They stopped in the entryway, where the butler was

instructing several of the footmen. The butler stepped away and bowed as he approached the duke. "Your Grace."

"Billings. I am to join Her Grace and Miss Allen in the pink parlor. Could you please wait a spell and then announce Lord Munsford?"

Oliver looked at the duke with a furrowed brow.

"It will go over better if it appears you have just come for a morning call." The duke nodded and waved Oliver to the side, as if this whole exchange was normal.

Oliver felt a tickle of uncertainty dance down his back. The duke was acting odd. "Your Grace, does Miss Allen know of our arrangement?" Oliver did not know if he hoped she did or didn't.

"Shearsby," the duke corrected; he gave a tentative smile. "Yes. She is aware of our agreement."

Oliver raised a brow, reading what the duke was not saying. "And she is not happy about it. That is why you think she will not accept my offer?"

Shearsby shrugged. "She was upset and acting rashly. I don't believe she truly intends to seek out a paid position rather than accept your proposal. I'm sure, now she has had a chance to think on it, she will be much more amiable."

Oliver watched as Shearsby turned and retreated down the corridor.

His stomach twisted. He did not know how he thought this would go over, but for some reason, he had supposed the lady would be amenable. Based on the rumors he had heard, she would not be receiving other offers. It was questionable if anyone would even hire her for the paid position she threatened to seek. She was completely ruined. And yet, the duke implied she would not welcome Oliver's offer.

For a brief moment, Oliver thought about leaving and not

calling on the lady. But again, such rash actions would surely put him at odds with the duke.

Oliver took a deep breath, tilting his head from side to side. The duke was right. He may as well get this over with. Perhaps it would not be as bad as Shearsby thought. Perhaps she would be amiable after all.

Billings cleared his throat and motioned with his eyes toward the corridor the duke had disappeared down. "If you will follow me, my lord."

Oliver nodded his head, but his stomach belied his calm exterior.

The butler opened the door and announced Oliver, stepping to the side to let him pass.

Oliver smiled widely, until he saw the frosty glare on the face of his soon to be betrothed.

A breath hissed through his teeth. Perhaps the duke was right, after all. Such was not the look of a lady about to become betrothed.

CHAPTER 5

Rose stood next to Lord Munsford, barely listening to the words coming from the Bishop's lips.

She took a stuttering breath. To be married in St. Paul's cathedral should have made her beyond happy. But she wasn't. She fluctuated between sad and angry, two emotions she had become intimately acquainted with of late.

The speed at which their marriage took place did not help her feelings. She had only learned of the agreement between the duke and Lord Munsford five days ago, and now she stood beside him in front of the Bishop of London. She had known the duke was anxious to be rid of her, but that he would be the one to pay for the special license hurt her pride.

A gentle nudge next to her brought her out of her musings. She looked at Lord Munsford who smiled at her and motioned with his head toward the Bishop.

The Bishop scowled at her. "Miss Rose Allen, wilt thou have this man to thy wedded husband, to live together after God's ordinance in the holy estate of Matrimony?"

What if she said no? Her stomach jumped at the thought. She glanced over her shoulder at Violet and the duke sitting on the front bench next to Lord Munsford's mother and sister. Her father stood at her other side, smiling as if he'd had some hand in bringing these nuptials to fruition. It would serve them all right, if she should decline.

Rose turned back to the front. No matter how hurt and angry she was at her sister and brother-in-law, even at her father, could she really do such a thing? She squeezed the stems of the small bouquet of flowers in her hands. Once again, it would not be Violet's reputation which would suffer. Rose knew she could not withstand another blow.

Lord Munsford nudged her again.

"I will," Rose said. That was it. She had done it.

She felt someone take her right hand and looked down to see her father pass it over to Lord Munsford.

Lord Munsford held onto her hand, gently squeezing it. She looked up into his eyes. What did she see there? She did not even know this man, and she was about to pledge to love him and take care of him in sickness and in whatever else should befall them in this life. Could she really do it? Could she promise God she would do all those things, when she felt nothing but indifference, or worse, anger toward this man? No, perhaps she was not angry with him, but rather the situation. The clarification did little to make her feel better.

Lord Munsford released her hand and looked at her expectantly. Rose stared back.

"You are to take my right hand now." He whispered to her, moving his hand closer.

Rose grasped his hand, mumbling her part after the Bishop.

Lord Munsford let go of her hand again, only to take it up with his left hand. He placed a ring on her fourth finger. "With this ring I thee wed, with my body I thee worship, and with all my worldly goods I thee endow—" Rose snorted. What worldly possessions? Was that not why he was here with her now? She noted a look pass over his eyes, but whether it was hurt or vulnerability or even anger, she could not say. But when her father cleared his throat next to her, she knew he was displeased with her.

"In the name of the Father, and the Son and the Holy Ghost. Amen." Lord Munsford's voice was quieter as he finished his speech. He did not meet her gaze, keeping his eyes trained over her left shoulder. Perhaps it had been a shadow of hurt she had seen in his eyes.

* * *

THE CARRIAGE RIDE was relatively quiet. Lord Munsford seemed content to play with his hat. Rose stared out the window. Her new husband was not much of a conversationalist.

The carriage came to a stop.

"We have arrived. It is not so grand as Heatherton House, but I hope you will find it comfortable."

"The company cannot be any worse, so you have that in your favor, sir."

His brow furrowed and Rose felt immediate regret at her snide remarks. He did not deserve her venom. After all, it was not entirely Lord Munsford's fault she was in this predicament.

"It looks very comfortable. I am sure it will do well enough." Rose frowned. Why did her words, even when she was trying to sound amiable, come out sounding cutting and rude?

She took a deep breath. Perhaps if she could rest, she would find herself in a better mood. Rose was glad she had declined the small gathering Violet had wanted to host following the wedding. Rose found she was in no mood for such festivities.

Lord Munsford stepped from the carriage and waited on the walk to hand her out. Rose noticed his tightly pressed lips as his hand released hers once she was safely on the sidewalk.

They walked up the stairs side by side in an uncomfortable silence. What did one say to a stranger whom you were now supposed to live with?

The door opened and a small woman smiled at them.

"Welcome home, sir." She dipped her head to Lord Munsford and then to Rose. "Lady Munsford."

Rose untied the strings of her bonnet and began to work the fingers of her gloves, surprised that the title did make her feel moderately better.

"I am Mrs. Finch, the housekeeper. Please let me know if I can assist you in any way, my lady."

Rose swallowed as she nodded. The title would take some time to get used to. It was odd. She had called herself Your Grace so many times leading up to her meeting the duke, she did not believe that transition would have been difficult. But this one? It all happened so quickly; she'd hardly had time to think on it.

"Mrs. Finch can show you to your chambers. My mother and sister should be returning shortly. They thought you may want a moment to get acquainted with the house before they returned."

Rose looked around. He had spoken the truth. This house could boast very little in common with the duke's townhouse. The entry way was small, with an unimpressive chandelier hanging in the center. Lord Munsford, it seemed, had also been truthful in his explanation of the family's financial difficulties.

"It doesn't appear there is much to get acquainted with, is there?"

Lord Munsford stiffened and Rose again felt, too late, the sting of her words.

"Yes, well, I am sure you are tired. I will leave you to rest. I have an appointment I must get to." He retrieved his hat and gloves from Mrs. Finch and walked quickly toward the front door. "I shall be back before mealtime."

Rose had not the time to reply before the door shut him from view.

Rose turned back to the pinched face of Mrs. Finch. "Please, follow me, my lady."

Rose's shoulders dropped. Not only had she earned the ire of her husband, she had also succeeded in angering the housekeeper. Rose growled at herself internally. Why could she not keep her thoughts to herself? It was going to be difficult enough being the stranger in this household; she did not need to have the servants against her from the beginning.

"I did not intend to offend," she stammered to the older woman as they made their way up the stairs.

The woman did not turn around or speak, only let out a harrumph.

They finally arrived at her chambers; Rose could scarcely wait to get inside and close the door on the events of the day. Every time she thought things could not get worse, somehow, they always seemed to do just that.

"Here you are, my lady." Disdain dripped from Mrs. Finch's tongue.

"Thank you, Mrs. Finch."

The housekeeper only dipped her head slightly. "Is there anything else I can do for you?"

Rose shook her head. "No. I believe I shall rest for a spell. If you will have my maid, Mary, awaken me in time to dress for dinner?"

"Of course." She turned to leave, and Rose felt a desperate need to mend the woman's opinion of her.

"Mrs. Finch."

The housekeeper paused and looked over her shoulder.

"Thank you. again."

Mrs. Finch shrugged slightly and sniffed, before turning back and resuming her walk down the corridor.

Rose breathed in a heavy breath and pushed her way into her bed chambers.

She flopped onto the bed, staring up at the ceiling. Little plaster flowers on a vine circled around the perimeter of the room. Rose lifted her arm, dropping it over her eyes. Her thoughts raced over everything that had happened today. The more she thought, the more her head ached. "Gah! Enough!" she shouted to the ceiling. "I cannot think on it a moment longer."

A small knock sounded on the door. Rose dropped her arm back over her head and onto the mattress. Was it Mrs. Finch come back to scowl at her some more?

"Come."

The door opened a crack; Lord Munsford's sister stood staring timidly at her from the corridor.

Rose sat up and tilted her head to the side to better see the girl. "You are Hannah, yes?" She had seen her at the church and been introduced ever so quickly.

Hannah nodded her head.

Here was someone who did not dislike her—yet. Perhaps if Rose was not her usual self, she could gain at least one friend. Rose stood up and walked to the door, motioning with her hand. "Come in, Miss Brandon."

She flicked her gaze down the corridor and then quickly scooted into the room.

Rose looked down the corridor but saw no one there.

Miss Brandon sat on a chair next to the window. "Mama told me not to bother you until you came down for dinner. But..." She paused and looked down at her hands. "I've never had a sister, or even a female cousin. I just could not wait that long."

Rose smiled and sat in the chair facing her. It had been a long time since someone had been anxious, even excited, to be in her company. "I am glad you came. We have not had any time to become more than properly acquainted."

Miss Brandon nodded as she bit her top lip.

Rose grinned. Until the girl overcame her shyness, it seemed it fell to Rose to initiate the conversation. "How old are you, Miss Brandon?"

She ducked her head. "Please, call me Hannah."

Rose nodded. "And you may call me Rose."

"I am not yet fifteen," Hannah said. "My birthday is in January —just after Epiphany."

"You are very lucky to come to London at such a young age."

Hannah shrugged. "It is my first time. Although, Mama says we may not do any shopping or go to the theater. I do not understand why London is all the rage. I find little to enjoy here." She sighed, her slight shoulders dropping dramatically. "I should rather be in the country riding my horse." Her eyes raised and caught on Rose. "Except now that you are here, I am very excited about that."

Rose laughed. "And what do you suppose I should do to entertain you? I cannot replace your horse."

Hannah giggled and then stopped, changing to a more lady like laugh. Her training for her come out had already begun, it seemed.

"No, I should think not. But I hope at least to have someone to talk with. Mama never feels well enough to talk with me. It is either her nerves or her head which are aching, and I only make them worse."

Rose felt her chest tighten. Her own mother had died long ago, but she understood the need and desire to confide in a mother. Perhaps it was something she and Hannah had in common.

"Well, I should enjoy talking with you, should you ever have the need."

Hannah clasped her hands together. "Oh, it is just as I always imagined! I already love having a sister."

Rose smiled. "I am glad to hear it." Rose stood and snatched a rug from the end of the bed. She only partially unfolded it, draping part of it over her lap and hugging the rest into her chest. "You said you were to stay for dinner? Do you often come to dinner with Lord Munsford?"

Hannah's brow furrowed. "Of course we do. We live here also."

Rose's eyebrows rose high on her forehead. "Oh. Yes, I suppose I should have considered that."

Hannah nodded. "Papa is gone." She leaned in closer to Rose. "I do miss Fernwood House. Though I should never tell Oliver such things. They think I do not know that Papa left us poor, but I do." A small frown turned down the corners of her mouth. "I don't know why they feel they must lie to me; I am not so daft as they think me."

Rose scooted her chair a little closer to Hannah and patted her hand. "I don't believe they think you a dolt, Hannah. I should guess they are trying to spare you the embarrassment."

"Perhaps." She gave a little shake of her head. "Even with as little as we have been out, I have heard whisperings about my father and Oliver. Maybe they just do not trust me to know the truth."

Rose gave Hannah's hand a little squeeze. "Let us make a pact with each other that we shall always be completely honest with one another."

Hannah squeezed Rose's hand back. "Yes, let's. I promise I shall always be truthful with you. It is what sisters do, is it not?"

Rose felt her throat tighten. "Yes. It is precisely what sisters do." Or that is what she had always thought.

CHAPTER 6

Oliver growled low in his throat. Why did someone have to be sitting in his favorite spot? There were other empty chairs scattered about the parlor in Brooks's, but he was in a foul mood and he wanted his chair or no chair at all.

He moved through the parlor into the billiards hall. Several gentlemen occupied the room, already in the midst of their games. One table remained empty at the far side of the room. Oliver grabbed a stick from the rack and moved to the unoccupied table, content to hit the balls about without an opponent.

"Ah, Munsford. I haven't seen you since you arrived in town." Mr. Penderton stood after he struck his ball, sending it rolling toward a corner pocket.

"Penderton." Oliver inclined his head but continued toward the end table.

Several men abandoned their games and followed Oliver.

"I understand you are to be married?" Mr. Penderton asked. He came to a stop beside Oliver's billiard table, his brow raised.

"I had heard the nuptials were to take place today." Mr.

Fairchild placed the wide end of his cue on the toe of his Hessians. "Have you already had to flee from the dragon?"

Several of the men laughed.

Oliver bristled slightly. "Actually, we were married this morning. But I am not come to escape. The new Lady Munsford," lud, that was going to take some getting used to, "was excessively tired. She asked to be left alone to rest until dinner."

Mr. Brown snickered. "I believe I shall add a new wager to the book—how many times a week Lord Munsford will 'not be hiding out' in his club." The men laughed again.

"That wife of yours, Munsford, may end up with an entire page in the betting book dedicated just to her." Mr. Penderton slapped Oliver several times on the back.

Oliver racked up his balls and straightened, leveling his gaze at Penderton and Lord Kent. "What, precisely, are all these wagers you speak of?" Did he even care? It was not as if the chit deserved his concern. She had treated him with nothing but contempt since first she laid eyes on him. Why should he concern himself with the tales being bandied about? A niggle of guilt wormed around in his stomach. *It is only concern for my own reputation.*

"Lord Peter Smyth wagered Lord Keeton you would send the chit to the country before a fortnight could pass." Mr. Fairchild formed a circle, touching the tip of his thumb to the tip of his middle finger. He swirled the narrow top of his cue around the circle. "I personally wagered Lord Markum it would take a month. You are a patient man, after all." He grinned at Oliver.

Lord Kent leaned over the table next to Oliver and knocked the tip of his cue into a ball, sending it spinning across the table. "You already won me my wager, good man. Many thanks."

Oliver scowled at Kent. "Oh? And just how did I do that?"

Kent leaned back against the wall. "I wagered the duke would not wait a full month before he foisted the baggage off on someone." He chuckled. "I didn't expect it to be you who would win it for me, though. Many apologies, but a win is a win."

"I am happy to have obliged you, Kent," Oliver said through gritted teeth. "I shall have to stay more apprised of the betting books in the future so as to not let it happen again." Oliver bent and lined up his shot, hoping they would return to their own tables if he started his game and ignored them all.

Kent shrugged. "I don't understand why you are so unobliging. It is not as if you were unaware of what sort of baggage you were getting."

"Ah, Munsford. I didn't expect to see you here." At the sound of the Duke of Shearsby's voice, the other men vacated the immediate area, returning to their own tables to continue their games.

Oliver smiled genuinely. Perhaps it would not be so bad to have a duke for an in-law. Even though the duke was new to society, he already seemed to instill a fair amount of fear in most men.

Lord Timothy was the only gentleman who stayed by Oliver's table, sitting in a chair in the corner. He was the only one who had not ventured a comment on Oliver and his misfortune of a wife. He stood when the duke approached, bowing slightly.

"Your Grace." Oliver dipped his head. The duke raised his brows and Oliver corrected himself. "Shearsby."

The duke looked at Lord Timothy. "My lord. It is good to see you again."

"Likewise, Your Grace."

Oliver's eyebrows raised, a slight smile forming on his lips. The duke and Lord Timothy were acquainted? Oliver did not know why that both surprised and pleased him. Perhaps it was because he liked both men very much and found he liked the idea of associating with them together.

The duke looked around, but there was not a cue to be found.

Oliver handed the duke his stick. "What brings you to the club, Shearsby?"

He shrugged. "Violet said she was tired. But I believe she was just making an excuse. She was not pleased with my role in securing your offer for Miss Allen—or rather, Lady Munsford." The duke leaned forward and took his shot at the balls. He straightened and looked about them. Lowering his voice, he continued. "In truth, I have felt a twinge of guilt myself. Not that I would take any of it back, but perhaps I could have handled things differently, or somehow better. Have you read the betting books?" He frowned for a moment before shaking it off. "But what is done is done. She will thank me in time, I am certain of it."

"I would not hold your breath," Oliver muttered.

"Oh? Pray, why not?" The duke looked genuinely interested, the barest hint of a chuckle sounding.

"My wife does not seem overly content with our lodgings, our conveyance about town, my title, or even me, for that matter." Oliver ran his hand through his hair. He knew he was not the catch of the Season, but he did not think himself as bad as his wife seemed to.

The duke put his hand to his chin, his forefinger extended up over his lips. "It will take time and I am sure a great deal of patience—mostly on your part, Munsford. But I believe she will come around."

Oliver wanted to believe Shearsby. He had never had romantic notions about finding a love match, but he had hoped to at least be cordial, if not friendly with the one he married. So far, Lady Munsford was anything but cordial or friendly.

Lord Kent and Mr. Penderton finished their game and returned their sticks to the rack. Oliver strode over and retrieved one of the cues. He leaned over and took his shot. Several balls skittered around the table, but he missed his intended ball altogether.

"It appears your head is not in the game, Munsford. Unless, you always play so poorly." The duke's head turned slightly to the side, his gaze measuring Oliver up.

Lord Timothy chuckled from the corner. "It is the former, Your Grace. I can assure you of that."

Oliver shrugged. He needed to do something. The current state of his marriage could not be tolerated. Perhaps if he made an effort, showed Lady Munsford some kindness—heaven knew she could use some kindness—she would soften toward him and allow a friendship to develop.

The duke handed the cue to Lord Timothy. "I find I am in no mood for billiards. I believe I shall return to Heatherton House."

Oliver nodded. He should probably think of returning home before too long, as well. But the thought of seeing Lady Munsford again had him placing the balls in formation for another round. His plan could wait another hour, surely.

The duke clapped Oliver on the back. "Give her time, Munsford. You will see she is not wholly bad."

Oliver didn't think the duke looked overly convinced of his own words. Perhaps he was trying to convince himself, as much as Oliver.

The duke turned to leave but stopped and turned back. "Oh, we would love to have you and Lady Munsford over for dinner soon. I shall send a card over tomorrow with details. Your mother and sister are invited, as well."

Oliver smiled. "Thank you, Your Grace. I am sure they will be most happy to accompany us."

The duke stared at Oliver for a moment, his mouth screwed up to one side, then he nodded decisively and continued out of the room.

Oliver leaned back over the table and struck the balls with his stick.

"Why did you not defend your wife to Kent and Penderton, Munsford? I thought you a better man." Lord Timothy's gaze held a look of both disappointment and confusion.

"What? And what was I to say, Tim? You heard them. Had I said anything, they would only have turned on me." Oliver took a shot. "Besides, what did they say that was not true?"

"Truth or not, she is your wife now. You could not have managed the likes of Penderton and Kent? Surely, you are not to be cowed by them. The Oliver Brandon I know would never have stood for it."

Lord Timothy and Oliver had been friends since their first year at Eton. The youngest son of a Marquess, Tim had never been one to gab excessively, choosing only to speak when he felt strongly about something. Which meant when he did speak, one should listen to what he said.

Lord Timothy stood up and smoothed the creases from his pants. "What would you have said had the same charges been leveled against your mother or sister? Would you have let those gentlemen say such things about them?"

Oliver swallowed hard. Tim was right. Oliver would never have allowed it and would likely have called the men out. His stomach burned. How could he ever claim to be Lady Munsford's friend if he would allow such things to be said of her?

Oliver twitched. He did not like sharing the same characteristics as Penderton and Kent. While Oliver had not said anything derogatory about his wife, he had done nothing to quell the rumors or wagers being made against her.

"What shall I do?" Oliver placed his hands around the top of the stick and rested his chin on top.

"I think you know what you must do."

Oliver shook his head. "Truly, I do not."

Lord Timothy returned the stick to its place and came to stand in front of Oliver. Tim placed a hand on Oliver's shoulder. "Perhaps if you return home, something will come to you on your ride back." He strode from the room without so much as a look back over his shoulder.

Oliver put the cue against the wall. Was marrying Miss Allen not supposed to have relieved the stresses in his life, rather than add new and more complex ones?

He took a deep breath and walked from the billiards room. His favorite chair by the window was now empty, calling to him to come and think.

Oliver sat down heavily. There was nothing he could do about the bets being placed—or was there? What if he placed a bet of his own? A seed of doubt settled in the back of his mind, even as he continued to think the plan forward. If he were to make a bet contrary to the others, perhaps it would send the message that he was in support of the new Lady Munsford.

Oliver twisted his head back and forth, working at the knot that had formed in his neck. It was not as if he had blunt to use for such a wager. But he did not intend to lose this bet, so what would be the harm?

He would begin to court his wife properly. Surely, the only reason they did not get on well was because they did not know one another. Oliver smiled. Perhaps things were not so bleak as he had originally thought. He pushed himself to standing and walked purposefully to the betting book, where Mr. Penderton and Lord Smyth were speaking in low tones. Both men looked up when Oliver approached.

Oliver noticed two new bets between the two men written on the page.

"You gentlemen seem fond of betting. How about a wager with me? Should I not get in on the wagers concerning my own wife?"

Penderton raised a brow. "Oh? And just what would this wager be?"

Oliver swallowed discreetly, not wanting either man to fully realize Oliver's trepidation. Although, perhaps if they did catch on, they would place a higher wager.

"I wager each of you four hundred pounds," both men's eyebrow shot up. "That my wife and I will not only achieve an amiable friendship, but an actual love match." *Love match?* Why in tarnation had he added that bit in? Oliver stopped himself from pounding his fist against his head.

Neither Smyth nor Penderton spoke for several moments, but Lord Smyth was the first to break the silence. "How can you afford such a wager, Munsford? Everyone is aware of the mess your father left for you."

Oliver bit the inside of his cheek. What was he doing? Had he not always prided himself on the fact he was not a gambler? Perhaps he should pull out now. He looked from Mr. Penderton to Lord Smyth. A smug smile slid across Penderton's face and Oliver's decision was made.

"I have just received a dowry of ten thousand pounds, gentleman. But if the sum is too steep for the likes of you..."

Both men cleared their throats before nodding. "No, of course not," they said in unison.

"But how are we to know if it is love or not?" Smyth squinted at Oliver.

Oliver clasped his hands behind his back. "Can one not see a look of love? I believe it should be quite obvious."

"But what is the time frame? We cannot have this go on for years." Penderton folded his arms across his chest, leaning back on his heels.

Oliver pursed his lips, thinking on how long he thought it would take him to accomplish such a feat. "The end of the Season."

Penderton nodded, followed by Lord Smyth.

"Very well, though, I doubt it would make a difference if we gave you until Christmas." Mr. Penderton laughed and nudged Lord Smyth in the ribs.

Oliver held out his hand. "You have yourselves a wager, gentlemen." He shook hands with them both before quickly writing the bet in the book. He gave the gentlemen one last nod then strode purposefully out of the parlor and down the stairs.

Oliver clasped the railing, afraid his legs would give out, as he thought about what he had just done. His shoulders stooped. Taking one long, deep breath, he stood up to his full height. It was time to start courting his wife.

CHAPTER 7

Rose took the last bite of her biscuit, the preserves and butter sticking to the sides of her lips. She licked at the sticky sweetness before wiping her entire mouth with her serviette. It was her first breakfast in days outside of her chambers. She had not even accepted the invitations—for there had been several—for them to dine at Heatherton with the duke and Violet.

She lifted her teacup to her lips as her husband walked into the breakfast room, with Hannah close behind.

"Ah, here you are." Lord Munsford smiled at her. He did that a lot of late. Rose wanted to believe he truly was happy to see her, but she could not see a reason as to why he would be. She had done nothing to earn his good nature.

Hannah bounced on her toes; her hands clasped in front of her.

"I have noticed you have not been out much of late. I hoped you might accompany me to the museum to see the Elgin Marbles."

Hannah's face broke out in a wide grin, her head nodding quickly.

A tickle of excitement formed in Rose's stomach. The marbles had only recently been moved to a room off the main gallery at the museum. The museum itself was something she had wanted to see when last she was in London, but she had never made it—after all, a museum was something only a bluestocking would be excited about—or so Miss Pulley had claimed. Things were so much different now. Rose need not worry about the opinions of society anymore.

"I did not plan to go out today." Did Lord Munsford's face fall slightly? Rose shook it off. Why did she care if it did? She shifted in her chair. It was not as if she could hide out for the remainder of the Season. She may as well experience what London had to offer. "But now you make mention of it, an outing could be diverting."

Lord Munsford's smile increased and traveled to his eyes.

Hannah squealed with delight and Rose found herself hard pressed not to grin along with the girl.

"I am happy to hear it. Shall we plan on departing just after one? Perhaps we could even stop at Gunter's for ices afterward."

If Hannah had been excited before, she was now almost in raptures.

"I will see I am ready and in the entryway by one. Thank you for the invitation, Lord Munsford."

He opened his mouth to say something but closed it and instead gave a slight bow. "Until one, then." He turned and strode from the room.

Hannah stayed behind, standing near the doorway, staring at Rose as she took another sip of her tea. "We shall have a wonderful time. Have you ever seen the marbles? I have heard they are quite fascinating."

Rose put her serviette on the table. Francis, one of the two footmen serving the family, stepped forward and pulled out Rose's chair. She nodded to him and mumbled. "Thank you, Francis."

As Rose left the breakfast room, Hannah fell into step with her. "Have you seen the marbles?" Her voice was more insistent than the last time.

Rose shook her head. "No. When I was in London several years ago, I had wished to see them when they were on display at the Duke of Devonshire's home, but I never seemed to find the time. This will be new to me, as well."

Hannah walked with Rose to her chambers following her inside.

Rose raised her brows at her forward sister-in-law.

Hannah's cheeks colored slightly. "Begging your pardon, Rose." She ducked her head and backed toward the door.

"You are welcome to stay, Hannah, but I am afraid you will be quite bored. I am to write to my father, so I will not be much of a conversationalist."

Hannah nodded, her shoulders dropping. "I'm sorry. I should have realized you were occupied and not have imposed."

Rose bit her lip and sighed. "Why do you not come fetch me at midday, and you can help me decide which dress I shall wear on our outing."

Hannah's eyes widened. "Oh, I should love to help." A giggle bubbled out of her throat as she grinned. "I shall leave you to your letter now." She turned and bounced out of the room, but not before poking her head back in. "Thank you, Rose. I do so love having a sister."

Rose's chest squeezed and a small smile hovered on her lips. She missed having a sister. It had been a long time since she and Violet had been close.

Rose shook her head and moved to the desk, dipping to smell one of the many bouquets scattered about her chambers, before preparing to write to her father about the mundane life she now led as a baroness.

* * *

At exactly twelve o'clock, a knock sounded at Rose's door. She sighed. Hannah was nothing if not punctual.

Rose pushed away from the writing desk and walked to the door, opening it just as Hannah raised her hand to knock again.

"Oh, you are awake. I was afraid you may have decided to rest, instead."

Rose shook her head. "Some days I feel as though all I do is rest." She opened the door wider, motioning Hannah inside. Rose eyed Hannah's dress. While it was clean and well kept, it was not the height of fashion. It was obvious she had not received new clothing for this trip to London. It should not come as any surprise, knowing what she did of her new family's financial difficulties. It was a practical decision. The money would be better spent in a few years when Hannah was presented and had her first Season.

Hannah must have detected the note of censure in Rose's gaze because her head drooped and she began to fidget with the lace at her neckline.

Rose mentally scolded herself. She must learn to school her features better or she would be in no better situation here than she was with Violet. Rose smiled, but the effort seemed too little and much too late. Trying to mend the damage she had already done, Rose walked to the corner of the room. "Your dress is very pretty. The color suits you very well." Pulling on the bell chord, she summoned Mary to come help her dress.

Hannah ran her hands down the front of the dress. "Do you really think so? I had thought the yellow may make me appear a bit sallow."

Rose shook her head. "Quite the contrary. It brings out the golden flecks in your eyes. You are quite lovely in it."

Hannah again fidgeted with her neckline, but this time a grin curved her lips.

Mary came in through the dressing room door, a dress in her arms. Rose shook her head. "No, Mary. Miss Brandon and I will be deciding on the dress I shall wear on our outing."

Mary's mouth twitched slightly downward, but it was the only indication of her displeasure. "Yes, my lady."

Rose flinched at the address. It had been nearly a week and still she was not accustomed to it.

Mary hurried into the dressing room ahead of Rose and Hannah, placing the dress back in the wardrobe.

Hannah moved over in front of the dresses and gowns, her hands brushing against the variety of fabrics. "This one is very pretty, is it not?"

Rose did not have a chance to answer before Hannah had moved on to the next one, awing over every dress she touched. Finally, she stopped at a soft lilac dress. It was perfect for an afternoon about town.

"This one." Hannah pulled it from the wardrobe and held it up to examine it. "I am sure Oliver will adore you in this dress."

Rose sighed. If only a dress could work such magic.

Hannah looked over at her. "Do you not believe me? I know my brother. Trust me, this is the dress for our outing today."

Rose smiled and motioned for Mary to take the garment from Hannah. "There you have it, Mary. Miss Brandon has made the decision."

The three left the dressing room, moving into her bed chambers. Rose sat at her dressing table, waiting while Mary readied the pins and combs.

Hannah stood beside the doorway. "I shall leave you to get

ready."

Rose turned slightly, looking over her shoulder. "Oh? I had thought we could talk as Mary fixed my hair."

Hannah's eyes widened and she nodded. "If you are amiable, I should very much enjoy it." She moved forward, sitting down on the end of the bed, at just the height that allowed Rose to see Hannah's face in the mirror.

Rose had no idea how much the girl could talk. Several times she questioned if Hannah might pass out from lack of breath. Rose could count on a hand how many words she had uttered in the time she was with Hannah preparing for their outing.

Finally, Mary stood back and moved to the bed to retrieve Rose's dress.

Rose moved her head from side to side, satisfied with the style Mary had settled on.

After moving behind a dressing curtain, Mary removed the morning dress and slipped the lilac dress over Rose's head. Mary quickly fastened the few buttons at Rose's back and then moved on to straightening the room.

Rose glanced at the clock. "Oh, my. It is nearly one o'clock. We must hurry. I should not like to keep Lord Munsford waiting." She grabbed her reticule and moved quickly toward the door, a small bubble of excitement fluttering about in her stomach.

Hannah followed along behind.

They reached the staircase and Rose slowed her steps, seeing Lord Munsford standing in the entryway below. He was speaking quietly to Hollings. Lord Munsford must have heard them, for he stopped talking and turned his attention toward them as they descended, a smile on his face. This one did not quite reach his eyes, until his eyes locked with Rose's. Then they twinkled merrily.

Curious.

Her stomach changed from a jittery excitement to flopping nervousness. *Stop being such a green girl, Rose. He is just happy you are not going to make him wait.*

She returned his smile with a quick grin or possibly it looked more like a grimace. She could not be sure what had actually transpired, her thoughts were so scattered.

"Ah, ladies. You both look lovely, this afternoon." He glanced back at the butler and nodded then extended his arms to Rose and Hannah. "Come, let us be off."

"Is your mother not to join us?" Rose cast a glance behind her, half expecting to see the dowager baroness following behind them.

Lord Munsford shook his head. "She cried off due to a headache."

He handed them into the carriage before stepping in and settling himself next to her. After a few raps on the side, the carriage set off down the road.

"Lady Munsford?"

Rose swallowed. His voice was deep, but rather pleasing. And the way he said Lady Munsford, almost made Rose forget she was generally angry. It sounded almost poetic. She looked away from the window, hoping he would not sense what she had been thinking. "Yes, my lord?"

He looked at her, his mouth opening and then shutting as it had in the breakfast room. He stared at her a moment before he spoke again. "Tell me, have you seen the marbles before?"

Rose did not believe that was his intended question. What had he been going to say before he changed his mind? She shook her head. "No. I was telling Hannah—" she stopped, feeling her face color slightly. She knew better then to use Hannah's Christian name when they were not alone. "As I was telling Miss Brandon earlier, when I was in London several years back, I had wished to see them, but the Season ended before I had the chance."

Lord Munsford smiled, giving a small but firm nod of his head, as if he had just decided something in that precise moment. "They are quite remarkable. I am happy to be the one to introduce you to them."

"And I am excited to finally see them."

He shifted and his thigh rested against hers, the heat from him warming her even through his pants and her dress. She knew she should scoot away from him, but the gesture was comforting.

The carriage pulled to a stop and their conversation ended for the moment.

Once both the ladies were out of the carriage, Lord Munsford led them toward the temporary room housing the great treasure. As they entered, a quiet stillness filled the air around them, as if the gods and goddesses there were demanding the respect they thought they deserved.

Rose clutched at the drawstring on her reticule as they stared at the frieze, walking slowly as they studied each piece of the carving.

"I've heard tell these carvings are representative of the Panathenaic procession." Lord Munsford's eyes never left the marble.

"Have you visited this exhibit before?" Rose looked at him from the corner of her eyes.

"I have. I cannot remember the number of times I have come to see these sculptures. I am quite fascinated by them." He took a step to the side, moving a few feet down the frieze. "The procession was only held every four years, when the citizens of Athens brought their goddess, Athena, new robes."

Rose nodded, more out of habit than understanding. Not that the information was dull; Rose was surprised how much her interest was piqued. It was only new, and she wasn't quite comfortable enough to ask further questions.

"If you look closely, you can see that the frieze is carved deeper at the top than at the bottom." Lord Munsford pointed toward the top of the frieze.

Rose leaned in to look up at the carvings from a different angle. "You are correct." She looked over at him, noticing for the first time the small crinkles around his eyes when he smiled. "Why do you suppose they did such a thing?"

He grinned like a boy about to reveal a great secret. "The frieze was located high on the wall in the Parthenon. They carved it in this way so the top could be seen as easily as the bottom, by those standing on the ground."

They moved past the frieze, walking around the statue of a woman dressed in gowns indicative of early Greece. Rose had seen similar drawings in a book she had read during her schooling. The woman looked to be carrying a bowl on her head and her arms had been broken off at some point in time. "Who is she?" Rose was not sure why she whispered the question, except that it felt right.

"I do not know her name, but she is a caryatid from the Erechtheion."

Rose's brow furrowed. "The Erechth--?"

Lord Munsford grinned. "The Erechtheion. It was one of the temples of the Acropolis. This caryatid was one of many that held up the portico."

"It is not a bowl she is carrying on her head, then?"

Lord Munsford shook his head. "No." He studied the sculpture. "Lord Byron has criticized Lord Elgin for stealing these from their homeland. I find I am of a divided opinion. If they were still in Athens, we would not have the pleasure of seeing them now. But I can also understand the value of keeping them in their native land."

This man was different than she had originally believed him to be. He was not nearly so dull, and even his unruly hair was not as unappealing as it had once been.

Rose and Hannah walked around to the back of the statue; both of their faces raised toward the ceiling. For one dressed so plainly, the statue was very beautiful. Rose could guess she was a goddess of some sort.

The two ladies moved to another set of sculptures. The first looked as if it may have been an angel, but its head, arms and wingtips had been broken off. Rose tilted her head to the side, looking around at the back of the statue.

Hannah let out a small gasp.

Rose jerked her gaze away from the marbles, focusing instead on her sister-in-law. Hannah's face was crimson, and her hand rested over her mouth, her head ducked.

"What is the—?" Rose glanced up at the statue in front of them and noticed a sculpted man, in an obvious state of undress. "Oh, my." Rose felt her face heat, perhaps not as much as Hannah's, but enough to indicate her embarrassment.

"Come, Hannah. There are others over there." Rose began to pull the girl away from the statue, when she knocked into someone.

Miss Carlyle took a step back, looking from Rose to the statue. She placed a gloved hand over her mouth, then reached out her other toward Hannah. "Miss Brandon. I see your sister-in-law's reputation is starting to tarnish yours as well." Miss Carlyle pulled Hannah toward her. "Come, I can see you home without any further disgrace befalling you." She turned narrowed eyes on Rose, glancing sideways at the statue. "I should expect nothing less of you, *Lady* Munsford."

Rose swallowed hard, her hands clenching at her side, unsure if anger or embarrassment took precedence. Her shoulder twitched slightly.

Miss Carlyle looked just over Rose's right shoulder, a reptilian smile spreading over her face. Rose turned slightly to see her husband standing just behind her. Had he heard the whole exchange?

His smile appeared tight; obviously he was embarrassed. He stepped forward and put his arm out to his sister. "I'm sorry, Miss Carlyle, but I cannot let you take Hannah away. My wife and I did promise to get ices at Gunter's after seeing the marbles." He then extended his arm to Rose, looking pointedly at Miss Carlyle. "Please, excuse us."

Rose tentatively took hold, allowing him to lead her away.

Once they were safely seated in the carriage and leaving the museum, Lord Munsford finally spoke. "I find I am looking forward to a cold ice. What of you, my lady?" His voice was altogether too happy and cheerful to be genuine.

Rose stared out the window but glanced discreetly at him from behind her bonnet. Did his face seem more pink than normal? She thought he looked at least slightly embarrassed. Whether it was for her or because of her, Rose did not know. Her chest tightened. Why did she hope it was the former rather than the latter? Rose sat up taller. What did it matter? It was not as if she desired his good opinion.

She took a deep breath, steeling herself against the lump forming in her throat. "I find I am no longer in the mood for ices today. If you would be so kind as to deliver me home first."

Hannah opened her mouth, but Lord Munsford shook his head, stopping her.

"Come, Lady Munsford. Surely once you taste it, you will change your mind."

"I said no, my lord," she snapped, not even turning her head from the window. She watched shops and then houses roll by, hoping she could make it to her chambers before her emotions came crashing down around her.

CHAPTER 8

O liver stood in front of the small cart of flowers, a young girl watching him expectantly.

Most of the flowers were obviously from the hothouse, which was not the most desirous; Oliver felt they did not smell so good as flowers grown out of doors in their natural season. But hothouse flowers were better than no flowers at all.

He perused the assortment on the cart.

"Have you decided yet, sir?" The girl watched him. "The lady must be very special, for all the flowers you have bought."

Oliver had purchased all the bouquets for his wife from this stand. It had the best variety of flowers he had found in London.

"Yes, she is," he said absently as he tapped his chin with his index finger. What did he wish to tell her with this bouquet? His eyes landed on the bright yellow clumps of goldenrod. Encouragement. Yes, his wife certainly needed encouragement. "May I get a few stems of the goldenrod, please?"

The girl nodded and selected the most vibrant of the stems.

Oliver smiled. It had taken a few purchases, but once the girl started recognizing him, she always made sure Oliver got the best blooms she had.

"Several of the red asters as well." Asters meant patience. Oliver did not know if the patience was for her or him, but at least one of them was in need of it.

"A very good choice, sir. The asters are especially pretty today." The girl gently pulled five stems of asters from the bunch and dispersed them among the goldenrod. The red of the asters made the yellow of the goldenrod stand out even more.

"A few of the white dianthus will complete it nicely." The final touch, sweet and lovely. Oliver looked at the bouquet with satisfaction.

Oliver grinned slightly. Sweet might be a bit of a bouncer, but lovely certainly did describe Lady Munsford. He had seen short glimpses of sweetness in her character before that dreadful Miss Carlyle had come upon them in the Elgin room.

"For two farthings, I can tie a ribbon round it, sir."

Oliver nodded. "Please."

She bundled the stems together and tied a pale-yellow ribbon around them, handing them to Oliver.

"That'll be a thruppance, sir."

Oliver put his fingers into the small pocket of his waistcoat and pulled out a few coins. He dropped them into the girls upturned hand and dipped his head to her.

She curtsied as he turned and walked back toward Leven Street and his rented townhouse.

The door opened as he approached. Hollings bowed as Oliver stepped through the doorway. "Welcome back, sir. I hope your walk was pleasant." He looked at the flowers. "It appears it was successful, if nothing else."

Oliver smiled. "Yes, indeed it was." He snatched up the post from the table and headed up the stairs toward his study.

"Hollings, please send a maid to my study to fetch these flowers for Lady Munsford. I should like to include a brief note with them."

The butler nodded as he bowed. "I shall send one straight away, sir."

Oliver entered the small room he called his study. It was a closet compared to the study his father had occupied at Fernwood House on St. James Street.

Oliver let himself indulge in a moment of frustration and remorse over the loss of his family's London home. Fernwood House had been in the Brandon family for nearly a century and in one bad venture, his father had lost it.

A knock sounded at the door and Oliver shoved the old memories away. "Come."

The door opened and a small maid stepped into the room hovering close to the doorway. When Oliver looked up from his desk, she was looking at the floor, but still she managed a curtsy.

"You were very prompt. I have not yet finished my note."

She continued to look at her feet. "I'll wait in the corridor, sir." Before he could object or consent, she slipped through the small gap between the door and frame and left the room.

Oliver stared at the door with a raised brow. How had she managed to squeeze through such a small crack?

He shook his head, bringing his attention back to the note. The flowers said everything he wished to say, but Lady Munsford would expect some sort of note to be tucked within the blooms. What could he say that he had not already said in the previous bouquets?

Munsford. Oliver looked at his name scrawled across the card. There seemed to be an overwhelming amount of cream-colored paper visible. It felt unfinished. He added a small *yours* above his name. His head tilted to the side. It was better, but still seemed to be lacking.

He sat down in his chair. Perhaps he should refer to something from their time yesterday. A breath fluttered his lips as it pushed out. Unfortunately, the events of yesterday now seemed tainted and marred by the harsh and unfeeling comments of Miss Carlyle.

A new thought struck Oliver and he scribbled it out before he changed his mind, filling the space above his name. *Please accompany me to the theater tonight.*

He stared at the card, then quickly pushed it into the bouquet. Walking quickly toward the door he thrust it into the maid's hands. "Please deliver these to Lady Munsford."

Oliver stepped back into his study and closed the door. He went to his desk to go over the books, but his head was not in it.

He kept thinking back on his note. What had possessed him to ask her to the theater? He knew what was likely in store for her should they go. Miss Carlyle was not the only vulture waiting to get their bit of flesh from his wife.

But what was he to do? He had already asked her. What if she said yes? Would an evening at Covent Gardens end in much the same way as their visit to see the marbles? Oliver ran a hand over his face. Why did he not think more where his wife was concerned? Or was it that he thought too much? "Thunder and turf." He ran his hand through his hair.

What he needed was to find someplace that was below the notice of most of society. Someplace they could go and not have to worry about Lord Kent and the others like him.

Oliver sat down in a chair next to the fireplace and picked up the newspaper, absently looking through it.

A knock sounded at his door and he dropped the paper to his lap. "Come."

The door slowly pushed open, the same maid he had sent with the flowers standing in the doorway.

Oliver waited for her to enter or at the very least step forward, but she did not. She just continued to stand in the doorway staring at him.

"Yes?"

She jumped slightly at his voice, then scurried forward and placed a folded note on the table next to him. Dropping a curtsy, she scurried back out of the room.

Oliver picked up the paper and unfolded it. Three words were all that was written. *No, thank you.*

What? She had turned him down? He had known it was a possibility, but he did not really believe she would do it. Why had she said no? Was it out of fear that another incident like the one with Miss Carlyle would occur or was it something to do with him? There was no explanation to lead him one way or another.

Oliver tossed the note back onto the table next to him and picked up his paper again. And to think his flowers had implied she was sweet. He forced himself to look at his paper, needing something to distract him. An advertisement in the lower corner caught his eye.

Aquatic Theatre, Sadler's Wells presents: The Spectre Knight.

Oliver stopped. He had heard of Sadler's Wells. The whole thing was supposed to be rather spectacular. It was popular and would no doubt be well attended; however, it was also known for its rowdier crowds. People such as Miss Carlyle would surely not tolerate such behavior. Oliver pushed himself from his seat and folded up the paper, placing it on the side table atop the note from his wife. He would purchase them tickets and convince Lady Munsford to accompany him.

OLIVER CLUTCHED the tickets in his hand. They were not the seats he had desired but considering his late purchase and the tightness of his purse, it was the best he could do. The man at the theater had assured him there were no seats in the theater in which one could not see.

It had not been lost on Oliver that the man did not answer his questions about the rumored rowdy crowds. Still, Oliver was excited to attend. Now he just had to convince his wife to attend with him.

Oliver bounded up the stairs, two at a time, knocking on Lady Munsford's chamber doors. "My Lady, I have something I wish to discuss with you. Are you about?"

When no sound came from inside and the door did not open, Oliver turned and went in search of his wife, or at the very least, someone who knew her whereabouts.

A footman stood in the small room just off the entryway where Hollings examined the silverware laying on the table. They both turned their attention to Oliver as he tromped down the stairs.

"Hollings, do you know where Lady Munsford is? She does not seem to be in her chambers."

The butler shook his head but turned his eyes to the footman who stepped forward slightly. "I believe she is in the back garden, sir. Or that seems to be where she goes most often."

Oliver nodded and turned in the direction of the back of the house. He stopped mid-stride and turned back. "We will be needing the carriage tonight. Please see it is readied."

Both men nodded and Oliver continued on his way to the garden.

He stepped outside and looked around. As far as gardens went, it was not terrible. The beds were weeded, and the hedges trimmed. But it lacked a certain sophistication that marked many of the gardens of the great houses in London. Again,

Oliver thought back to Fernwood House. It had beautiful gardens.

Oliver sighed. If only he had more money. He could employ more than one gardener and see that more variety of plants were grown. Not that he didn't appreciate roses. He did. But there were so many other plants and flowers available.

Clasping his hands behind his back, he returned his attention to looking for his wife. This garden was not large by any standard, so it should not be a difficult task.

He stepped down the single step onto the small stone terrace. At the back of the garden, under the shade of a tree, Lady Munsford sat on a bench, her shawl pulled tightly around her arms.

Keeping his eyes on her, Oliver walked to her. She looked up when his foot stepped on a twig, snapping it in two.

"Lord Munsford. You startled me. I was not expecting you."

Was that anger in her voice or just surprise? They had not even been married a fort night and had spent very little time together before the nuptials had been taken. He wished he knew her well enough to know her expressions and her intonations.

"I did not mean to impose. I only came to try and convince you to come with me tonight. I am certain it will be most diverting."

A shadow passed over her eyes and she shook her head. "I believe it best if I keep to the house." She fiddled with the fringe on the edges of her shawl. "I should not like to do any more harm to Hannah's reputation than I have done already."

Why did his sister get to be called by her Christian name? Oliver had wished to ask for her to call him Oliver on several occasions but had decided against it each time.

"Then you have nothing to worry about. Hannah shall not be accompanying us tonight. She and my mother have made other plans. I believe one of mother's friends is having a card party—a

73

bunch of matrons getting together to gossip and complain, I am certain. She shall be taking Hannah with her. So, you see, there is no reason for you to refuse my offer."

Her rigid body made Oliver brace for a heated refusal and he took a slight step back to prepare.

"Very well. If Hannah shall not be affected, I will join you. I have already sullied *your* reputation, so what could be the harm?" Her voice was not quiet, yet there was still a note of timidity and uncertainty. At least he thought as much. But perhaps he was completely wrong.

He clapped his hands together. "I am happy to hear it! We shall have a splendid time. Just you wait and see." Why was he smiling like an idiot just because his wife had consented to attend the theater with him? He grunted quietly. How else was he supposed to respond? Especially when he had been positive she would decline. But she had not declined. Perhaps this marriage would not be as the betting books predicted after all.

CHAPTER 9

W hy did I agree to this? Rose sat in the carriage opposite her husband and smoothed her hands down the front of her gown for what must have been the hundredth time. She moved her fingers to her throat, rubbing her mother's pearls, quietly counting each one until her heart slowed to a normal pace.

The carriage rolled to a stop and Rose looked outside. This was not Covent Gardens nor Drury lane. Where exactly were they?

After stopping and starting several times, the door finally opened, and the footman stood ready to hand them out.

"Are you ready, my lady?"

Rose closed her eyes for a moment, caressing her pearls one last time. Nodding, she stood, then ducked down to go through the door. Lord Munsford stood at the bottom, a smile on his face, his hand extended to her.

Rose placed her hand in his and stepped from the carriage. A small tickle of heat raced up her arm as he gave her hand a quick squeeze before letting go. Rose looked over at him, but his gaze was focused on the building before them. Candles burned in dozens of lanterns affixed to the face of the building.

"What is this place? I thought you said we were going to the theater." Rose walked a little closer to him as several men pushed their way to the front of the line.

"We are. This is the Sadler's Wells Theater. Have you not heard of it?"

Rose's brow furrowed and she shook her head. "No. Should I have?" The building looked as any other building in London. It was the crowd of people she was more distracted by. The ladies and gentlemen appeared to be in a line going through a different door than she and her husband were headed for. The people in line with them were more roughly dressed and many, it was evident, had already made a visit to a nearby tavern.

"I confess, I have never been before, but I understand it is very diverting. They have constructed a large glass case on the stage which they fill with water. The entire show takes place in the glass case." His eyes alighted with excitement and Rose found it impossible for her excitement not to rise with his.

"Truly? How is such a feat to be accomplished? I find I cannot even imagine it."

Lord Munsford nodded his head. "I agree. I am most excited to see how they constructed it."

They were pushed along until they were finally standing at their seats. Rose gave a slight sigh, relieved to be settled.

This was not what she'd had in mind when Lord Munsford asked her to accompany him to the theater, but it did look interesting. The large glass case full of water was larger than anything she could have imagined.

Rose looked around the theater, noticing several boxes along the upper levels. She recognized several of the people sitting there from the other line entering the building. Rose's nose twitched as the smell of sweat and spirits wafted from the two men seated next to her.

She pressed a handkerchief to her nose, grateful for the smell of rose which lingered on it. She turned toward her husband, deciding even with his unruly hair, she still preferred to look on him than any of the other people surrounding them.

As she opened her mouth to speak, she spotted a bright color from the corner of her eye. She glanced up and saw Lord Kent sitting in one of the boxes above, a bright yellow waistcoat making him stand out from the crowd. He caught her eye and smirked, just as she looked away.

"Pay him no mind. He is a complete nodcock." Lord Munsford picked up her hand and gave it a small squeeze. Her heart picked up its pace once again.

Rose glanced over at her husband. His mouth was set into a tight line.

They were saved from having to speak more of Lord Kent or anyone else sitting above, when men began to blow out the candles in the lanterns on the side walls. The large chandeliers remained lit, but the sides darkened slightly. A rustle of sound rippled over the audience as people settled into their seats and prepared for the show to start.

Rose watched the events playing out in the large tank of water, miniature replicas of the British navy sailing back and forth. Rose held her breath as small children, playing the roles of Spanish sailors, were dropped into the water, struggling to stay afloat among the waves.

The men next to her shouted vile curses and insults at the French and Spanish ships. Rose looked at them with barely contained disgust. Did the men not know how to properly behave in the theater? And these men were not the only ones. The whole of the crowd on the floor left much to be desired. They were loud and unruly.

Perhaps it would have been bearable had they been seated above, where it seemed the more civilized patrons sat.

Rose glanced over at Lord Munsford and he smiled. Then he winked. Rose's brow furrowed. Was her husband like these louts surrounding them? Had the man to her left not winked at her also?

The battle in the water finally ceased with a victory by His Majesty's Royal Navy. The crowd erupted in applause. The men next to her jumped to their feet, whistling and shouting again.

Lord Munsford stood and offered a hand to Rose. She glanced up at the boxes again, as she stood. Why she did it, she could not say. But immediately her gaze landed on Lord Kent. Rose had not noticed before that Miss Carlyle was on his arm. The two spoke to each other, their eyes never leaving her face, then laughed at some joke they shared. Rose's face burned with embarrassment. It was bad enough to know what they had said about her before, but how would they use this sighting to further scandalize her name and that of Lord Munsford?

Rose reached up and fingered her pearls. What did she care of Lord Kent or Miss Carlyle?

She closed her eyes a moment, grasping hold of the pearls to give her strength. One...two...three.... Her breathing slowed. Hopefully, she would not have to endure seeing them outside while they waited for their carriage.

Lord Munsford reached over and grabbed hold of her arm, pulling it and the pearls away from her neck.

Rose gasped, frantically trying to grab the pearls before they fell to the floor. "What have you done?" She yelled at him. Dropping to her knees she scrambled to pick them up before they rolled down the slight incline of the floor.

Lord Munsford turned and swore as he saw the pearls rolling

toward the front of the theater. He dropped down next to her, reaching as fast as he could before they rolled out of reach.

Rose sat back on her heels, the string and loose pearls cupped in her hand. She stared down at them, quietly counting what she held.

"Can you tell if any are missing?" His voice was quiet, barely discernible above the noise of the crowd leaving the theater.

"Five." Rose choked on the lump in her throat. Tears spilled from her eyes. "There are five pearls missing." Another bout of big, wet tears made long streaks down her cheeks. The more she stared at the pearls in her hands, the faster the tears came.

An awkward hand settled on her shoulder, which only served to make her cry harder. Sobs now joined the tears, shaking her whole body. She had been put aside by her betrothed in favor of her sister, sunk to the lowest level of humanity, been shunned by society, and married a stranger who only wanted her for her money. Through it all, she had tried to maintain a degree of dignity and decorum. But this was it. Not only was her mother's necklace ruined, but five of the pearls were missing.

Lord Munsford scooped the pearls from her hand.

She glared up at him. "What are you doing?"

"I thought if I put them in my pocket, perhaps we could keep from losing any more." His face looked confused. Did he not realize what he had done?

Something bumped her foot. Rose looked back at the man standing next to her, just as his glass tipped. Ale ran down her neck and back. Rose dropped her head into her hands, no longer caring who or what was around her. Her tears stopped, being replaced instead with an all-encompassing numbness.

She knelt there until the noise of the theater gradually faded. Gentle hands helped her to her feet. An arm went around her waist, but Rose paid it no mind.

Without realizing how it happened, she found herself stepping from the carriage in front of their townhouse. Lord Munsford helped her up the stairs. She heard him shout to Mrs. Finch. He then helped her up the stairs and turned her over to Mary, who met them in the corridor outside of Rose's chambers.

"What happened, sir?"

"I inadvertently pulled her necklace from her neck. We were unable to recover several of the pearls."

Mary gasped. "Her mother's pearl necklace, sir?"

Lord Munsford swore again.

Rose knew she should be outraged at her husband's language. But she did not care.

"I had no idea. It is no wonder—" he trailed off.

Mary put her arm around Rose's waist and guided her toward her chambers. "I shall put her to bed. I am sure she will be much recovered in the morning."

"Truly? You believe she will be well?" If Rose had been more about her wits, she may have believed he sounded worried about her.

"Leave her to me, my lord. I will see to her." Mary sat Rose on the bed and moved to shut the door. Rose watched him put what was left of the pearls in Mary's hand. He continued speaking to Mary, but she could not hear what they said. It was just as well; Rose did not think she could manage anything else today. Maybe even forever.

CHAPTER 10

Oliver slipped from the house before anyone but the servants awoke. The streets of London were quiet as he stepped up into the Munsford carriage.

Sitting down, Oliver rubbed his hand over the worn velvet on the cushions. This carriage had been the peak of luxury and fashion a decade ago. Now it was worn and held very little spring. His father had ordered a new carriage, but when Oliver had learned of their new financial reality, he had canceled the order. As the carriage bounced along the streets of London, Oliver felt the slightest regret over his decision.

He stopped briefly, arranging to pick up a small bouquet of purple hyacinths on his return trip. It was a far cry from the apology she deserved, but it was all he could do for now.

A short time later, the carriage pulled into the stable yard of Sadler's Wells and Oliver stepped down, happy to see the theaters manager, Mr. Dibdin, waiting in the piazza.

Oliver extended his hand. "Thank you for agreeing to meet me."

Mr. Dibdin nodded. "Your note was vague. What is it I can do for you?"

Oliver folded his arms across his chest. "My wife's pearl necklace broke inside the theater night before last. We were unable to account for all the pearls before we left. I was hoping I might come in and see if I could find them?"

Mr. Dibdin narrowed his eyes at Oliver, as if trying to assess the truthfulness of his request.

Oliver lifted a brow, challenging the man.

The theater owner nodded. "Very well. I will not be able to assist you. I have to ready the theater for our performance tonight."

Oliver unfolded his arms, dropping them to his side. "I should not assume to impose on you in such a way. I can manage the task on my own." He tipped his head slightly to the side, eying the man. Oliver did not know if the man would pocket a pearl, even if he were to find one. But he need not find out. "If you will just show me to the theater, I shall make my search."

Mr. Dibdin nodded his head as he extracted a ring with several keys dangling from it. "Please, follow me, sir."

Oliver fell in behind him, closing the door tightly after him.

The foyer was dark, and it took a moment for Oliver's eyes to adjust. Mr. Dibdin walked over and lit a candle from the banked fire in the grate. He proceeded to light several more in the sconces along the wall. Soon the foyer was filled with flickering light.

Mr. Dibdin took his lighting candle and moved toward a set of doors. He withdrew the key ring once again, inserting a key into one of the handles and opening the house door.

He held the door open with his body; his back leaned against it. "Here you are, my lord. I am afraid I cannot offer you the benefit of the light from the chandelier. Most of the candles are burned down to the nub from last night's production." He did light several candles in the sconces on the wall. The theater was no longer cast in darkness, but it was in no way well lit.

Oliver squinted across the seats. How would he ever find the pearls without more light?

Mr. Dibdin motioned toward the middle of the room. I will be replacing candles. If you should be in need of me, I will be within a shout."

Oliver nodded. "Thank you, sir. I appreciate you allowing me to search. The pearls are very special to my wife. She was most upset to have lost them."

Mr. Dibdin's face softened slightly. "Women folk usually are upset by such things. The floor has a slight incline to it. I should think you would want to start your search in the front." He gave a slight shrug. "Although, I can't say that no one picked them up last night."

Oliver sighed. That had been his worry as well. He had asked Mr. Dibdin to allow him to come yesterday, but the man had not been available to meet until today. Oliver had paid for a ticket to the show last evening but had only found one of the pearls resting against the front of the stage. Which meant the other four were either stuck somewhere between where they had been seated in the middle and the front row. Unless they had been spotted and picked up by other patrons.

Oliver walked to where they had been seated two nights prior and stared toward the stage, trying to figure the path the pearls may have taken.

He then went row by row, dropping down to his hands and knees, searching any gap that looked to be even close to big enough to house a pearl.

After four rows with no success, his spirits sagged. What if this endeavor was for naught and he was unable to locate the pearls? He supposed he could purchase four more pearls to replace those they had lost, but that would cost money he most certainly did not have—money he could not possibly take from the funds he had received upon marrying his wife. Additionally, pearls he bought would not have the same meaning and significance as those that had belonged to Rose's mother.

Oliver sat back on his heels, rotating his aching shoulders. He had to do whatever he could to find the pearls. If he must, he would run an ad in the Times and prevail upon anyone who had picked up the pearls to return them.

Oliver dropped back to his knees and began to search the fifth row. With every row, the search took in wider territory. Halfway down the row, Oliver caught a glint of light. He felt his way the rest of the way over and to his delight found a creamy white pearl, nestled between a knothole in the wood and a floor beam.

A happy laugh bubbled out as he dropped the pearl into his watch pocket.

"Am I to take it you found something?" Mr. Dibdin looked down at Oliver from a ladder reaching high into the chandelier hanging over the auditorium.

"Yes, I found one. I need only find three more." The success spurred him on to a quicker pace. Three more rows and he found a second pearl. An excitement squeezed in his chest. Two more. Surely, they were still here.

But three more rows with no new finds and Oliver's excitement ebbed. He was so close. He only had one row to go until he reached the front. It seemed unlikely that he would find both pearls in such close proximity to each other. But he refused to give up now.

He reached the end of the row and stood up to move to the next one. He rubbed at his knees with one hand, in part to dust them off, but also to sooth the soreness. He reached a finger inside his pocket and ran it over the smooth pearls inside, using them to spur him on to finish the task.

He walked to where he calculated the pearls path could have been and dropped to his knees one last time. It was darker here than it had been on the rows farther back as there were fewer sconces this close to the stage. Oliver ran his hand over the wooden slats of the floor, using his hands more than his eyes. He neared the end of the row, and his search, when his hand slid over what seemed like the hundredth knot in the wood. But something smooth filled in most of the hole, moving when Oliver brought his finger back and slid them over it again.

He leaned closer to the floor, his eyes adjusting and seeing the difference between the dark brown of the wood and the shimmery cream of the pearls.

Oliver nearly cried. Two pearls lay in the knot. The last two pearls. Now he could take his wife's necklace and have it repaired.

Carefully, he used his fingernail to lift the first pearl out of the knot, dropping it safely into his pocket. Then he lifted the last one out, rolling it back and forth between this thumb and forefinger. "You and your little friends have caused me a great deal of trouble." He placed the pearl and the tips of his fingers to the bridge of his nose. Closing his eyes, he whispered a thank you. It seemed the Lord had looked down on him today.

Oliver walked out of the row and made his way to the foyer. Mr. Dibdin was no longer on the ladder under the chandelier. Oliver hoped to find the man before leaving, so he could offer him his thanks.

Mr. Dibdin was pulling a handful of playbills from a stack and placing them on several short pillars.

"Thank you for your help, Mr. Dibdin."

He looked up from his task. "Did you find them all?"

Oliver smiled and patted his waistcoat pocket. "Indeed, I did.

My wife will be most happy." At least Oliver hoped she would. Although, he truly had no idea what made her happy. He had never actually seen such a mood from her. He had glimpsed it briefly in the Elgins room. But it had left almost before it had begun.

"Capital. Glad to hear it." He resumed placing playbills about the room but looked over his shoulder as Oliver turned to leave. "Do come back and see another show, sir. Our shows are unlike anything you will see elsewhere." There was a hint of disdain and Oliver guessed he was referring to his competitors over at Covent Gardens.

Oliver placed his hat atop his head. "You can count on it." He pushed out the door and onto the piazza, the brightness of the sun not hitting him until he stepped off the walk and waited for his carriage to come around.

The sun was high overhead. Oliver put a hand above his eyes, blocking out the sunlight. Just how long had he been inside the theater?

He looked over toward the river, noticing his driver, Devins, fishing over the railing.

Oliver shook his head and strode over, putting his elbows on the railing next to the man. "Having any luck here, Devins?"

His driver jumped and looked over, nearly dropping his pole into the river. He quickly yanked the line back, winding it up quickly as he took several steps back. "Yes, my lord...I mean, begging your pardon, my lord," he stammered before giving a quick bow and jogging away.

Oliver stared out over the murkiness below. Gentle ripples stirred the water as it traveled around several determined plants growing out into the river.

The carriage came rolling out of the yard and Oliver lamented that he had to leave. It was peaceful watching the water, even if the location didn't have a pleasant smell.

James hopped from the back of the carriage. His eyes looked droopy and tired, his hair disheveled with a few bits of hay sticking to it. He opened the door for Oliver but said nothing. Oliver suspected James's voice would only incriminate him more.

Raising a brow at him, Oliver climbed into the carriage and sat down, stretching his legs out in front of him.

He took a pearl from his pocket, as the carriage lurched forward. He stared at it, trying to imagine his wife's face when he showed it to her.

Oliver grinned when another idea stuck him. Would it not be better to see her face when he placed the whole necklace about her neck? Surely, such an action would bring a smile to her face at long last.

CHAPTER 11

R ose sat in the chair facing the window, an unfinished and rather uninteresting sampler sitting in her lap.

She had scarce seen her husband since the disaster at the theater two nights before. He had been gone the whole of the morning. It was past midday and he had yet to make an appearance. It seemed he was either busy in his study or out somewhere. Rose sniffed loudly. Or at his club. But then why did she care where he was occupying his time? It was not as if she desired his company.

A form came into view on the sidewalk outside the townhouse and Rose leaned forward to get a better look. Her shoulders dropped when a stranger walked in front of the window and continued past the house.

Rose picked up the sampler, poking the needle up and down through the fabric several times, but paying it very little heed. Her gaze often flicking to the scene outside.

She had not received a bouquet of flowers this morning. While she did not necessarily enjoy the ritual, she had become used to it. Her chambers smelled like a garden.

The door behind her creaked open and Rose took in a deep breath. Could they not even afford to oil a squeaky hinge?

Rose looked over her shoulder and saw Hannah and her mother enter the morning room. Rose sucked in a quick breath. She had lived in the Brandon townhouse for nearly a fortnight and had managed quite successfully to avoid the Dowager Lady Munsford. Rose could not put into words just why she did not wish to spend time with her mother-in-law. Perhaps it was because doing so would make this whole charade seem real. It appeared as though her good fortune had finally run out.

Hannah looked around before spotting Rose in the chair by the window.

"There you are. We've been looking everywhere for you. When Oliver returns, he thought it would be diverting to see the menagerie." Hannah clapped her hands together. "Does that not sound delightful? I have heard tale there are lions and tigers and even an elephant." She bounced on the balls of her feet.

Rose shook her head. "I think it best if I remain at home." Another form outside jerked her attention back to the window. Her heart skittered slightly when she recognized the slight bounce in his step.

Lord Munsford stepped up onto the small landing before disappearing through the doorway.

"Oh, good. Oliver is home, Mama." Hannah turned her eyes back to Rose. "If I cannot convince you to come, perhaps he can."

The dowager settled herself quietly into a chair by the fireplace. Even without looking in the lady's direction, Rose could feel the older woman's gaze. This must be where Lord Munsford got his penetrating stare. Rose stared down at the fabric in her hands, forcing herself to concentrate on the stitches.

She glanced at the door to the corridor several times, wishing Lord Munsford would come in and save her from the awkward silence now hanging in the room. But the door remained closed.

Rose growled as she realized she had misplaced several stitches. She pulled the thread from her needle and began pulling the errant stitches out.

"You enjoy sewing, Lady Munsford?" the dowager asked from across the room.

Rose nodded half-heartedly. "I suppose it is entertaining enough."

"Hmmm..."

Hmmm? What exactly did that mean? Rose wanted to look up. Wanted to see what expression was being leveled at her, but she was afraid of what she would find.

"Does any woman truly enjoy needlework?" her mother-in-law continued. It felt like less of a question than a commentary of some sort. Although, Rose did not fully understand about what.

A hint of a smile crossed Rose's lips. "My sister seems to enjoy it. But she is fond of many such activities."

Her mother-in-law plucked a flower from the vase sitting on the table at her elbow. "I have only known dull people to like stitchery. Tell me, Lady Munsford. Is your sister dull?"

What a question to ask of a relative stranger. Rose ventured to look at her mother-in-law. The woman still stared at Rose, but she was surprised to discover a smile, rather than a frown, on the dowager's face.

Rose looked curiously at the older lady. "I should not suppose Violet is dull." Conniving and treacherous, perhaps. But not dull. "She is also very fond of music and plays no less than four instruments quite proficiently."

The dowager's brow creased. "And what of you, Lady Munsford? What are you fond of?"

Thankfully, the door opened and Lord Munsford entered the room. He instantly smiled. "Ah, all the lovely ladies in my life in one room." He held flowers in both hands.

He gave a small bouquet of white carnations and yellow tulips to his sister, bowing slightly as she giggled with delight.

He then moved to his mother giving her a bouquet of pink roses with white carnations. The Dowager smiled sweetly up at Lord Munsford. "Thank you, son." She held the flowers to her nose breathing in the scent. "You make it easy to smile."

The larger bouquet he then handed over to Rose. "And for you, my dear."

My dear? What did the sentiment mean?

Rose looked down at her flowers. Her bouquet contained purple hyacinth, hazel, and white daisies. It was an oddly pleasing combination. Rose looked up, studying him. Why did he bring her so many flowers? And why so many hyacinths? Perhaps they were a particular favorite of his. She lifted the hyacinth to her nose, closing her eyes as she smelled the sweet scent. "Thank you."

Lord Munsford clapped his hands together. "I thought perhaps we could visit the menagerie this afternoon. What say you all?"

Hannah moved to his side. "I think it a fabulous idea. I need only put my blooms in some water, and I will be ready." She turned her head toward Rose. "Rose does not wish to come with us. Please, Ollie, you must convince her. I am sure it will be great fun."

His cheeks pinked slightly at the intimate name. "Perhaps you could find Mary and have her see to Lady Munsford's flowers and I will stay and try to persuade her to accompany us."

Hannah reached for Rose's flowers.

"Would you see to mine, also, dearest?" The older Lady Munsford stood and placed her flowers in Hannah's already full hands. "I shall endeavor to help your brother convince Lady Munsford. I am certain she cannot refuse us both."

Rose looked back and forth between her husband and her mother-in-law. Neither looked stern or unpleasant, yet they did look unyielding.

Rose sighed. It seemed she had little choice in the matter. She would be forced out into society. "Oh, very well." She removed the sampler from her lap and placed it in the basket next to her chair.

"I know Hannah is ready to leave. But I should like to have tea first." The dowager turned to Lord Munsford. "Unless, of course, you wished to go out for tea."

Lord Munsford bit his lower lip. "I think tea before we leave would be best. After all, I would hate to miss out on Mrs. Benton's scones." Lord Munsford's eyes widened. "It smells as if she made the cheese ones today. They are my favorite."

Lady Munsford looked expectantly at Rose.

Was she angry Rose had taken her place as mistress of the house? Rose felt in an odd position, knowing how she would feel were the roles reversed, yet still not wanting to give up her place as mistress. She had not become a duchess. Was it too much to ask to remain mistress in her own home?

The lady continued to watch her steadily.

Rose swallowed. Gah. If the woman wished to prepare the tea, what did Rose care? The twisting in her stomach told her she cared very much. Still Rose pulled the key from her wrist and extended it to her mother-in-law. "Would you prefer to prepare the tea, my lady?"

"Pish. You are the mistress of the house, my dear. You need not cow to me, or to anyone." She moved to the corner of the room and pulled the bell cord.

Rose placed the key back on her wrist, her hands clutching in front of her. Why did she seem incapable of getting anything right? Perhaps it was fate which had stripped her of the title of duchess, rather than Violet, for Rose was obviously not up to the task.

Her stomach burned. No. It was Violet's fault. Her cheek gave a twitch. She rubbed at it several times until it stopped.

Just as Lord Munsford had predicted, the scones were indeed, of the cheese variety and were delicious. Rose could understand why they were his favorite.

He leaned back in his chair and patted his stomach. "I am in need of a walk. Shall we be off to the menagerie?"

Lord Munsford extended his arm to his mother and to Rose, but his mother shook her head slightly and took a step back.

Once bonnets and gloves were retrieved and fastened, they stepped out into the bright afternoon sun. But the sun's rays on her face were short lived as they stepped up into the carriage.

Hannah chattered non-stop until the carriage stopped. Rose looked out the window. This was not the Tower of London.

"Did I misunderstand? I thought we were going to the Tower menagerie, Lord Munsford."

He took a deep breath. "I do wish you would call me Oliver." The words rushed out of his mouth and his gaze flicked nervously about the carriage, repeatedly returning to her face. The longer the silence stretched the more his eyes bounced around.

"Very well. Then you should call me Rose." Was she ready for such intimacy? She watched his shoulders relax and his ready smile returned. Perhaps she was not ready, but from the expressions which crossed his face, it appeared this was important to him and she could not bring herself to disappoint. He had been very kind to her, and she could give him this kindness back.

"You were only partially wrong, Rose." Gooseflesh erupted on her skin. Had anyone ever said her name with such reverence and warmth? Rose rubbed her hands slowly over her arms to push the tiny bumps away.

"We are going to the menagerie, just not the Tower menagerie. We are at the Royal Grand National Menagerie at the Exeter 'Change."

Rose eyed him suspiciously. "I have not heard of a menagerie here."

"It is not quite as well known as the Tower, but it is equal in its magnificence. Or so I have been told." He exited the carriage, waiting on the walk to hand her out.

When she reached his side, he held his arm out to her. She placed her hand atop his forearm, and they took several steps forward, waiting for his mother and sister to be handed out by the footman.

Rose felt suddenly jittery. Something had changed with the use of their Christian names.

Hannah came up beside her. "Are you not excited, Rose?"

Rose nodded, not sure what her voice would sound like should she answer just then.

They entered the arcade on the street level, climbing the stairs to the second floor. Rose stared, placing her gloved hand to her nose. Surely the tower did not smell so bad.

At least a dozen cages lined the walls, while several smaller ones sat up high. Birds of different sizes and colors sat in small cages on tables under the windows on the opposite side of the room.

A tiger paced back and forth behind his bars, snarling when someone stepped too close.

Monkeys swung around in the smaller cages at the top, chattering and at times throwing things through the bars into the small crowd gathered below. Rose shuttered, not wishing to find out just what the furry creatures were casting out. They scooted closer to the lower cages, lest they be in the path when something else was thrown from above.

Their little group stopped in front of the next cage.

"What is that?" Hannah asked as she pointed at the large gray animal.

"It is a rhinoceros, I believe." Rose looked for some sort of sign to give them information, but she saw nothing.

Oliver handed her a paper. "Here, this may help."

Rose read over the descriptions. "It says that this rhinoceros is from India. It is considered one of the largest of its kind."

They walked past the cages of the emus and kangaroos before stepping into another room, similar in appearance to the first, except at the back, bars reached from floor to ceiling. A large elephant stood inside.

Rose continued to read as they moved in front of each cage. "Here is a tapir and a hippopotamus from the New World."

There were lions and leopards and a panther. When they reached the elephant, the large beast walked toward the front of the cage. Rose looked into his large brown eyes with long eyelashes. "Hello, Chunee," she said, reading the elephant's name off the paper in her hand. She tilted her head to the side. "He looks unhappy, do you not think?" Rose looked up to Oliver.

He shrugged. "I can't say I know what an unhappy elephant looks like."

"Look in his eyes. There is sadness there." Rose felt for the animal trapped in the cage. She understood what it felt like to have no options or say in how you lived your life.

Oliver squinted up at Chunee. "I believe you may be right, Rose." He gave a slight chuckle and Rose glanced over at him, angry he should be laughing at the animal's pain. "I read an account made by Beau Brummel after he visited this place several years ago. He said the elephant was so well behaved, he wished Chunee were his butler."

Rose gave a small smile as his mother and Hannah laughed

with Oliver, but Rose could not laugh at the poor beast. They had too much in common for her to make light of his situation.

As they moved on to the next cage, Oliver placed his hand atop hers. He gave it a gentle squeeze. Rose could almost hear the apology in his gaze as he looked down at her.

She glanced over her shoulder at Chunee once more. Perhaps she did not have as much in common with the elephant as she originally thought. For she had hope there may actually be some happiness in her future.

CHAPTER 12

"You asked to see me, sir?" Mary stood with her head bowed in front of Oliver's desk.

"Yes, Mary. I wondered if you might do something for me, or rather, for your mistress?"

His wife's lady's maid eyed him with a degree of skepticism. "Of course, sir. How may I help?"

"I am in need of Lady Munsford's pearl necklace—the one that broke the other night. I would like to have it fixed for her. I know it is very special and I should like to see it restored."

Mary stood silent, watching him through her lashes. It was almost as if she did not believe him. Curious. Why should she have cause to doubt his honesty?

"Why do you not ask her yourself?"

Oliver smiled. "I wanted it to be a surprise." He held out several of the pearls he had found the day before at Sadler's Wells. "Do you not think she would enjoy a surprise?"

Mary seemed to think for a moment before she nodded her head. "Yes. I believe she would. But Lady Munsford does not leave the house oft. She keeps to her rooms. How shall I get them for you?"

Oliver put a finger to his chin and tapped. What could he do to get her away from the house? Mary was right. Rose did not usually leave willingly.

"Ah, I have just the thing. She and I shall take a turn about Hyde Park. It is a lovely day and it should give you enough time to fetch the pearls."

Mary nodded. "Is that all, sir?"

"Yes, yes. You may go."

Mary turned to leave but stopped when Oliver called her name. She looked back over her shoulder.

"Thank you for your help, Mary. I shall not forget it."

Oliver grinned widely. He had been thinking since he found the lost pearls how he would go about getting the rest of the pearls from Rose's room without her knowing. Mary was the perfect solution. Now he need only convince Rose to join him on a walk.

He looked at his watch. If they left now, they could finish their walk before the fashionable hour brought out the crowds wanting to be seen. Oliver wished to avoid those people like one wished to avoid the plague. He had already witnessed their cutting remarks to Rose on several occasions. And as her husband, the duty fell to him to protect her from such hurtful comments.

He went to the morning room first—it seemed to be one of her preferred rooms—and found her immediately, torturing her poor sampler. Her mouth was screwed up to one side as she worked roughly at a knot in her thread. She seemed overly agitated and Oliver shrank back for a moment. He had seen her bad temper enough to know he did not desire to encounter it again.

Rose tossed the sampler into the basket at her side with a huff.

Oliver watched her quietly as her chest rose and fell. Her eyes closed and she took several long slow breaths.

His chest tightened. She truly was one of the most beautiful women he had ever laid eyes upon. Had it not been for her tarnished reputation, he should never have ended up with a lady such as she. Perhaps he did have something to be grateful to the *ton* for.

Rose's eyes opened and she spotted him staring at her. "What are you gawking about? I am not one of the animals in the menagerie for you to stare at and study."

Oliver tensed. perhaps he shouldn't be thanking the members of the *ton* just yet.

"I have come to invite you to take a turn about Hyde Park with me. It is lovely out and I thought you may enjoy some air." His earlier excitement began to dim.

"It is several hours yet before the fashionable hour. Why should we go now?"

Oliver swallowed. He did not wish to come right out with it. "I find I do not like the crowds. If we go now, we could be home before most of the people have even arrived." He clasped his hands behind his back.

Rose sat still for a moment, staring at her tightly clasped hands in her lap. Without saying a word, she stood up. "I shall fetch my bonnet and gloves, then."

Oliver nodded. Why was nothing with this woman easy? She seemed so wholly disappointed. Or perhaps she was sad? He did not know how to label her emotions, except that she was not happy. He did not like it. Even angry Rose was preferable to what she was now.

He strolled to the entryway, retrieving his hat and gloves from Hollings. Rose stood nearby, tying the ribbons of her bonnet under her chin, a silent tension filling the air between them.

Without a word, she allowed him to lead her to the waiting carriage and hand her up.

"Thank you for the flowers you sent this morning, but you need not buy me a bouquet every day. I am sure you have much better things to spend your money on."

Though her words expressed thanks, her tone did not. Did she not like the flowers? While she had not openly gushed over them as Hannah always did, Oliver believed he had seen a hint of a smile on several occasions after she received them. Had he been wrong? "Nonsense. They do not cost so much, and I like to be able to help the girl who sells them."

Her brow crinkled slightly.

This morning's bloom, while a single stem, made him feel vulnerable. What if she did not feel the same? He had felt yesterday as though they had reached a level of friendship. She had allowed the use of their Christian names, which Oliver had been sure she would adamantly refuse. He had seen a tender side of her in her concern for Chunee, the elephant. This morning, the simple yellow rose had seemed the most appropriate for their new budding friendship.

But now Oliver was doubting all of his previous notions. Perhaps he should have given a calla lily or another white hyacinth, telling her of her beauty. But it seemed so superficial to keep dwelling on her surface characteristics only.

They drove the remainder of the way in silence. When finally they stopped, he helped her from the carriage. She placed her hand atop his arm. Oliver's brows raised slightly in surprise. Given her current mood, he had not believed she would allow him to have her hand. Gah! He wished he knew her well enough to understand what she may be thinking and feeling. How could he help to change those feelings if he was not certain what they were?

While she allowed him her hand, the rest of her body was stiff and rigid. She walked with her shoulders straight and her chin lifted. "I am sorry."

Oliver looked down at her. "For what are you apologizing?"

"You need not think me ignorant of your intentions. I am perfectly content to stay at home, rather than have you take me out to obscure places at obscure times."

Oliver came to a halt and looked down at her in confusion. What the deuce was she speaking about? "What?"

She looked straight ahead. "Come now. I am not daft. I know the reason you took me to Sadler's Wells rather than Drury Lane or Covent Garden. Or to the Exeter 'Change Menagerie rather than the Tower. And now this walk in Hyde Park? At a time when no one will see us?" She took in a quick breath of air. "You do not desire to have your friends and other members of society see you out with me. I know your reputation must have suffered by our marriage."

Oliver removed her hand from his arm and put both his hands on her shoulders, turning her to face him. When she stared over his shoulder, he took his finger and gently turned her head, forcing her to look into his eyes.

"Is that what you think? That I do not wish to be seen with you?"

"What other explanation could there be? But you need not worry. I understand. I am relieving you of your duty to scurry me about town to see the sights. I am content with our townhouse and back gardens until the Season is over and we return to the country."

Oliver shook his head. "I did not think you completely daft, until this moment."

Rose's eyes widened with anger and Oliver almost felt relief to see the fire burning there. At least she looked as if she felt something.

"Yes, I have done these things to keep you away from the *ton*—" He put a finger to her open lips and continued. "Not because I am embarrassed by you, but because I am embarrassed by *them* and their complete lack of decorum. I have seen how some treat you. I have heard what they whisper. You have braved it well, but you should not have to be exposed to it time and again. I want you to see what London has to offer, but without the threat of public disdain."

Rose's head tilted to the side, studying him.

She took a step forward and in one swift fluid motion, threw her arms around him, hugging him tightly, her cheek pressed hard against his chest. "Thank you," she whispered.

Oliver's breath caught in his chest as surprise and pure enjoyment overtook his brain.

Her hold loosened and Oliver's brain cleared. He put his arms around her, pulling her back to him and resting his chin on her head, slowly breathing in the smell of roses. He felt her body rise and fall with each breath. This was right and good. Hope blossomed in his chest.

Moments later she took several steps back, releasing him and dropping her arms to her side.

Oliver wanted to pull her back but resisted. "It is I who should apologize for making you believe what you did. I should have made my intentions clearer. I will try to be more forthcoming in the future."

Rose shook her head. "No. I should not have assumed as much."

Oliver put his arm out and she laid her hand on top, resuming their walk again. Oliver pulled her hand around his arm, as he had at the menagerie.

A satisfied grin spread across his face when he felt her squeeze his arm and move a little closer to him. "I find, of late, it is easier for me to assume the worst in any given situation."

"I believe that is understandable. You found yourself in a difficult situation through no fault of your own. I imagine it is hard to believe anyone could be sincere in their kindness toward you."

Her steps slowed and her body sagged. What had happened to the relief of moments ago?

"Perhaps," was all she said, and they continued the rest of their walk in silence until they arrived back at the carriage.

Oliver settled in beside her. He wanted to pick up her hand and hold on to it while they drove back to the house. But given her sudden change in mood, he was worried such an action may send them back to their less than cordial acquaintance.

As happy as he was by their walk, he was equally confused. When she had hugged him, he had thought for certain something was developing, but then their conversation had turned, and it seemed to have put a damper on her mood.

She sat quietly next to him, but from the corner of his eyes he watched a number of emotions flit across her face.

What if she were regretting her earlier actions? Oliver knew he had felt something, a shift of some sort, in his feelings for her. What that entailed he was not certain, but he knew something was different. Different for the better.

However, her feelings were a complete mystery to him. And watching her puzzle over whatever was currently going through her mind only made Oliver more uncertain.

He ran a frustrated hand through his hair. Never had a woman confused him so completely as did this woman he called his wife.

CHAPTER 13

Rose did not know why she felt so disobliging. After learning what Oliver's motives had been yesterday on their walk, she should have felt happier. But her underlying feelings of inadequacy had only increased since their walk. It had all started when he had told her he found her behavior perfectly justifiable.

But why? He was right. What she had been through would make anyone distrustful.

Rose grunted softly. If one could not trust her own sister, who could she trust? Her cheek twitched.

She gave the bow on her bonnet one final tug and made her way toward the back of the house. She stepped down into the garden, the gravel pathway crunching beneath her feet. Oliver had asked her to join him for a picnic under the large beech tree at the back. Rose loved that tree. She did not know precisely what about it she loved. Maybe it was because the breeze blew the sweet scent of the rose bushes past it. Or perhaps it was the shade it provided in the growing heat of spring. Maybe it was because it was so far away from the bustling London streets, that she was able to hear the simple fluttering of the leaves. Whatever it was, it was her favorite spot in the garden.

She walked to the back, finding a large rug spread out on the ground. Oliver was nowhere to be seen. Rose dropped to her knees and sat on the ground, straightening her dress around her.

A breeze blew past, picking up the curls at the side of her cheeks. Rose breathed in the scents of flowers and moist dirt. If only the rest of London were this lovely. She could not say she had loved her time here this Season—or even enjoyed it—but there had been moments. Several events had made her situation bearable and at times even happy.

The image of her hugging Oliver in the park yesterday drifted to her mind. Her cheeks heated when she thought of how untoward she had behaved. But he had not seemed to mind and had even embraced her back. How long had it been since someone had held her close as Oliver had? In that moment, all the terrible things that had happened to her—because of her—melted away and she felt safe and loved.

Rose shook her head. Not that she believed Oliver loved her or she him. But still, the embrace had been pleasant.

She took a deep breath, trying to calm the butterflies swarming in her stomach. She would be glad to get back to the country. Rose frowned. To which county would she be going? She realized she did not even know where the Brandons hailed from.

Oliver dropped down on the rug next to her, bringing her attention back to the garden. He had a large hamper beside him and if possible, an even bigger grin on his face. "My apologies for keeping you waiting, my dear. I just could not decide between the berry scones and the buttered apple tarts."

There it was again. *My dear.* Was he trying to tell her something? Rose leaned forward to peer into the basket. "What did you decide?"

Oliver laughed, snapping the lid closed. Almost hitting her nose.

She jerked up, her eyes wide and her mouth open.

He waggled his eyebrows at her and she felt her anger subside. "Both. I hope you are hungry. I believe Mrs. Poole misheard me and thought I said we were picnicking with the whole of Prinny's Blue's." He opened the lid and began to withdraw several serviettes of food, placing them on the rug in front of them.

Rose gaped. "How are we to eat even a fraction of this?"

Oliver chuckled. "I think it impossible. When we finish, we can invite my mother and Hannah out to join us." He looked at her and winked. "Or return the hamper to the kitchen and let Mrs. Poole distribute the leftovers."

Rose snatched a small sandwich, taking a small bite as she looked around them. "What county will we be retiring to after the Season?"

Oliver glanced up. "Caddington Abbey is in Rutlandshire, near Oakham." He glanced up at her. "Have you been much in Rutland?"

Rose shook her head. "No, never that I can recall. Will you tell me about it?"

"Rutlandshire is truly the best county in all of England."

Rose smiled. She could argue that Cheshire was the best. But she did not see the point. She would certainly never convince Oliver of its truth, just as he would never convince her.

"There are many rolling hills with lovely valleys in between." He looked at her and shrugged. "I can see I am not doing it justice. You will just have to wait and see it for yourself. I hope you will love it as much as I." He plucked a leaf from a nearby plant, twirling its stem between his thumb and finger. "I had not planned to discuss such matters at present, but as you have brought it up. I was hoping we could talk, make a plan as it were, for your dowry."

His cheeks colored up and Rose could tell he was embarrassed to have to broach the subject.

"I should wonder at you asking me at all." Did not most men feel they were entitled to spend their wife's money any way they pleased?

"It is your money."

She shrugged. "That has made no difference to other men for centuries."

"I am not like most other men." Oliver smiled.

A notion she could not argue with. Oliver was, indeed, like no other gentleman she had encountered. "You find me at a disadvantage. I know nothing of Caddington. It will be difficult for me to make educated decisions."

"Perhaps we could start with the greatest need. Then wait until we return to Rutlandshire to make any further decisions."

Rose put her hand on the rug next to her, leaning her whole body to that side. "Where do you believe we should start?"

Oliver brought his knee to his chest and wrapped his arms around it. "The tenant cottages. Many are vacant because they are in disrepair. I believe if we could get them fixed up properly, we could get tenants in before fall."

Rose switched her lips to one side, squinting as she thought. No one had ever asked her opinion on matters of such import. She felt pressure to perform well. "But that will not give tenants time for a harvest before winter sets in. It is doubtful they could earn enough money to pay rent through the winter months."

Oliver let out a frustrated sigh. "Now you see my dilemma. This should all have been done months ago. But I was not aware of the whole situation then."

Rose sat up straight and reached a hand over, placing it on his arm. Did she dare voice her idea? Would he make light of it and disregarded the notion? "What if we do not charge the tenants rent until the cottages are repaired. They would need to live in the cottages while the repairs are being made, but they could plant crops now and have enough time to harvest them before winter sets in."

Oliver dropped his knee back down and turned to face her. "We would not be collecting rent for several months. Can we afford it?" He was sincere in his questions, giving Rose the confidence to proceed.

She shrugged. "We are not collecting rents now. But this way, we will be collecting rent at a minimum for half a year longer than if we fix the cottages first." She nodded her head. "I think this is our best option."

Rose braced herself for his dismissal.

Oliver looked pensive before giving a firm nod. "I believe you are correct." He studied her. "You have a very shrewd mind, my dear."

Rose grinned, her chest tightening. No one had called her shrewd before, nor had anyone taken her advice on something so critical.

"I shall send word to my bailiff immediately and tell him to start work on the cottages and find new tenants."

Rose picked up an apple tart and took a bite, unable to quell the excitement in her stomach. A comfortable silence settled over them as they continued to eat. Rose looked around the garden, because if she looked at her husband, he would surely see how much she was affected.

While this garden was rather plain in comparison to others she had seen, she still thought it lovely. Perhaps because it was her garden. How was it she had never seen any real beauty in nature before?

"I wish you could have seen the gardens at Fernwood House." Oliver's voice became wistful.

"Fernwood House?" Rose thought for a moment. She had heard Hannah mention the name before, but she did not know what it was.

Oliver nodded. "It was our London home, until recently."

He looked almost forlorn. Was he going to cry? Rose watched him closely, trying to spot any moisture about his eyes. "What happened to it?"

Oliver looked up, meeting her gaze and she knew.

"You had to sell it to help pay the debts left by your father." Her voice was low and quiet. She was not the only one who had suffered this Season.

Oliver put the apple tart he was eating back on the serviette, wiping crumbs from his pants. He chewed the pastry exaggeratedly, as if it were dry and sticking to the top of his mouth "Yes. The estate is not able to be sold, so in that we are protected, but Fernwood was not so fortunate." His eyes raised to meet hers. "I should have liked to live in Fernwood with you—have our children run about its halls."

Rose felt her cheeks heat, but Oliver seemed not to notice.

"But it is a part of the Brandon history now, not its future."

Rose looked back out to the garden. "How was it different than this garden?"

Oliver snorted. "How is it not different?"

Rose chuckled. It was such a boyish sound to make.

He paused for a moment, his eyes traveling over her face, stopping briefly at her eyes and then her nose. They stopped at her lips. "You are quite lovely when you smile as you are now."

Without thinking, Rose ran her tongue over her bottom lip, biting softly.

Oliver swallowed, his Adam's apple bobbing. "There—" He cleared his throat, pulling his gaze up to her eyes. "There is no comparison. Over a hundred different kinds of plants and flowers cover the ground, all blooming at different times of the year. Trees are scattered throughout, some flowering, while others weep over to the ground. The garden is never, except in the depths of winter, without color. There is even a fountain." Oliver gathered up the remaining food and put it in the hamper, waving to Francis who was standing to the side of the terrace door. He walked quickly toward them and took the basket from Oliver.

"Please return this to the kitchen."

"Yes, my lord." Francis nodded and bowed.

Oliver pushed himself to standing, dusting off his pants and stretching out his shoulders. He put a hand out to help Rose and she placed her hand in his. The same feeling of safety and right-ness she had felt yesterday in the park enveloped her.

Was she giving too much trust, too much of herself to him? It scared her. What if his affections were not genuine? She jerked her hand out of his. A chill went down her spine. Certainly they would not be sincere, if he knew the truth.

Nervously running her hands down her skirt, she smoothed out the wrinkles. What had he done to lead her to believe he was not in earnest? She looked up at him as he stared down into her face. There was not the slightest look of deception there, only a look of confusion.

She turned and tucked her hand through his arm, hoping the small gesture would help to mend any hurt she may have caused by removing her hand so hastily.

They set off at a leisurely pace through the gardens. Rose looked up at him. Could he see she was afraid? See she had opened herself up, allowing him to hurt her if he so chose? Rose looked at the gardens. "What would you do to this garden, were you able to change it?"

Oliver placed his hand over hers, his thumb moving slowly

over the top of her wrist. She wanted to pull it away, but it felt so nice she could not do it.

He pointed to a spot not far off. "I think a small wall fountain right there would be lovely. It is more about the plants, though. I would infuse more color." He picked up a white rose bud from a nearby bush. "Roses are lovely..." he smiled at her, raising his brows quickly, "in every form." He turned his attention back to the bud he held between his fingers. "But the rose is very singular. There are so many plants and flowers that could add such depth." He sighed. "Perhaps you need see it, in order to fully appreciate and understand my meaning."

Rose wished she could see the finished garden, if for no other reason than to see Oliver's face as he walked within it. "I am sorry we will never see your plan come to fruition here. It sounds lovely." She sighed. "And peaceful."

They walked around the path, coming back to the large tree they had started under. Oliver seemed content to take another turn, so Rose continued with him.

"Is that why you buy so many flowers?" It seemed the most logical answer for all the bouquets he purchased. She had never seen a man buy so many and in only a few weeks' time. Her bed chambers were beginning to look like a hot house. "Is it because you no longer have them in your garden? Buying them is the only way you can get the same effect as the garden at Fernwood?"

Oliver paused and looked at her. His brow creased and he opened his mouth, but then snapped it closed quickly.

He wished to tell her something, but for some reason he was holding back. "I guess, in part. My mother loves flowers. My grand-father was vastly interested in botany. He started many gardens around their modest estate. Most of the family found his studies boring, but my mother, she was a willing listener. She has taught both Hannah and me everything we know about plants."

He smiled, but his gaze was fixed on the garden before them. "As long as I can remember, we have had flowers everywhere, in the garden and in the house. When my mother married my father, he allowed her to work with the gardener, planning and planting anything she desired. While the house on Caddington is not so grand, the gardens surrounding it are. Every morning in the summer and fall my mother goes to the garden to pick flowers. She replaces the expired blooms in the house or sometimes just creates new arrangements. But most often she will walk about the paths, talking to her flowers as if they were her children."

Rose gave him a sideways glance, a brow raised in question.

Oliver chuckled. "She does not believe them to be her children. Just speaks to them as if they are."

Rose nodded, understanding at least partially what he was saying. She thought back on her own mother. It had been years since she had recalled the memories of her mother sitting on the bench beneath the honeysuckle trellis. While her mother did not talk to the plants, she did sometimes sing. When Rose had asked her why she sang to the flowers, her mother told her she was not singing *to* the flowers, but *because* of them. They made her happy and that is what urged her to sing.

"My mother was similar, in a way. Honeysuckle was her favorite. So much so that my father sent to London for a honeysuckle fragrance, so she could smell it always."

Oliver swallowed hard, his face softening while he stared at her.

Rose stopped, pulling her hand from his arm. Why was he looking on her in such a way? It made her jumpy and nervous.

Oliver's voice stuttered when he spoke. "How long has your mother been gone?"

Rose reached out and plucked a blade of tall grass, tearing it into slivers along its veins. "Just over eight years." She sighed. Sometimes it felt like forever.

While her mother had always been closer to Violet, Rose knew her mother had loved her. Her mother had taught her to play the piano. Rose had never loved music as her mother and Violet did, but she did love the time her mother spent at her side, whispering the directions into her ear. Oh, Rose missed those times. Times when they had been a family, when they had been happy. "Papa was never the same after she died."

Oliver placed a hand at her elbow, urging her forward. "At least you had your sister."

Rose let out a bitter laugh. "Oh, yes. What would I have done without Violet?" Her hands fisted and she folded her arms to hide them from Oliver. "I would certainly be a duchess now had it not been for Violet." She muttered it under her breath, but from the stiffening beside her, she knew Oliver had heard.

Oliver stopped short, moving away from her. The hurt in his eyes was evident and Rose felt a twinge of guilt. But she pushed it aside. Why should she feel guilty? She had been the one wronged.

Her cheek twitched and he lifted his hand, rubbing the backs of his fingers over it. He took a deep breath and schooled his features. "I can see how you could lay some blame at her feet for your current circumstances."

Some blame? Rose laughed mirthlessly. Violet was solely responsible for Rose's current circumstances.

"But even you must see the duke and duchess have a love match. Would you have taken that away?" Oliver's tone was quiet.

Rose's nostrils flared slightly. Why did everyone ask that question? She wanted to scream at him, but she remembered her decorum. "Yes, I would have. I certainly tried. But it all came to naught." Rose shook her head. She should have known better than to leave her future up to Mr. McPhail. How had she expected anything more from the third son of a gentleman? Or perhaps she should not have waited so long to take action.

Whatever her error, the plan had failed miserably. Instead of marrying Rose, when his beloved Violet disappeared, the duke had gone after her. Raced all the way to Scotland to save Violet. Rose's throat tightened, remembering how angry the duke was when he learned of her part in the plan.

They came around to the terrace and Oliver stopped. "You look tired, my lady. Perhaps you should go inside. I will go and fetch the rug." His face no longer held an easy, relaxed expression. His lips pressed tightly together, and his eyes darted, looking at everything but her.

Rose did not miss the absence of her Christian name.

He turned away from her, walking quickly to the back of the garden.

Rose unclenched her fists as tears of frustration and anger and guilt pooled in the bottoms of her lids. *This is all Violet's fault.* She squeezed her eyes shut. *No. This is my fault.*

CHAPTER 14

Oliver walked past the flower girl on his way home from the club. It was the first time in more than two weeks he had not stopped to buy flowers. But after yesterday's fiasco in the garden, Oliver did not feel inclined to give his wife flowers. He did not know what to say with them and she would not understand what they meant. Did he send her yellow carnations to show her his disdain? Perhaps a dispassionate hydrangea or an indifferent candytuft?

Oliver shook his head. Therein was the problem. He did not feel disdain, or indifference. He felt completely opposite of dispassion, or he would not be so hurt by her remarks, by her obvious disregard of him. She felt she had married beneath her.

"Sir," the flower girl called after him. Oliver stopped and turned back. Just because he was not buying flowers for his wife, did not mean he should not buy them for his mother and Hannah. They, at least, would appreciate the sentiment.

Oliver looked over the selection, picking several orange roses, white carnations and a lilac for the center. Sweet smelling flowers for a sweet, enthusiastic, young lady. For his mother he selected a simple bouquet of pink roses.

Dropping the coins in the girl's hand, Oliver turned to leave when his eyes caught on the purple carnations in the back of the cart. It would serve Rose right if he purchased them for her. After all, she was nothing if not capricious.

"Did you be needing anymore, sir?"

Oliver shook his head. The gesture would be lost on her anyhow, for he was certain she had no understanding of flowers.

He walked into the house and sought out his mother and sister. They were sitting in the parlor, Hannah reading a book and his mother stitching on a baby rug.

"Good day, mother." Oliver leaned down and placed a kiss on her cheek. She looked at him questioningly. They were not an affectionate family, but he did not see the harm in doing it this once.

He handed over the bouquet of roses to her and she smiled. "They are lovely, dearest. Thank you."

"And this one is for you, Hannah." Oliver made a grand bow in front of her, extending the flowers to her. Hannah giggled, just as he knew she would. He was a little sad to think that society would proper that giggle right out of her, far sooner than Oliver would like.

A rustle of fabric from the other side of the room brought his eyes upward. His wife stood from her chair, her eyes bouncing from the roses in his mother's hands to the bouquet in Hannah's. Stopping on Oliver's obviously empty hands. She gave a very discreet nod and walked toward the door.

Hannah shoved her flowers into his hands. "Give her mine, Oliver. I am not in need of flowers today." Her whisper carried across the room.

Rose stopped. "No, Hannah. I am certain he chose each bloom specifically for you." She turned back and continued out the door.

"Why did you not buy her flowers, Oliver? It was most rude of you." Hannah scowled at her brother. Apparently, she was going to take Lady Munsford's side.

"Hannah, you should not speak of things you know nothing about," Oliver snapped.

Hannah shrank back, sitting down in her chair, a pout on her lips.

"Oliver, you need not take your frustrations out on your sister." His mother held the flowers up. "Dearest, please take these and get them into water. You can see they are already starting to wilt."

Hannah narrowed her eyes at Oliver as she walked past to collect her mother's bouquet.

Once Hannah was out of the room, Oliver's mother patted the seat next to her. "What has happened? I thought you were getting on quite well, of late."

Oliver shrugged. He did not wish to speak to his mother on such topics, but this was hardly something he could discuss with Lord Timothy. Perhaps the duke would understand, and possibly even have some insight, but Oliver did not feel inclined to share such information with him, either.

"I believed we were also, until yesterday."

His mother continued her sewing. "What happened yesterday to make you question?"

Oliver told her of their picnic in the garden and the lovely time they'd had together. When he got to the part where Rose's mood shifted so drastically, his mother put her sewing down into her lap. "You were hurt by her words."

Oliver shook his head. "No."

She looked at him with a bland expression.

"Well, yes. I was hurt by her dismissal. But I was also disturbed by how angry she became. And over nothing that I can figure out."

She picked up her sewing once again. "What were you speaking of when she changed?"

Oliver sat down in a chair, watching his mother calmly placing her stitches. "We were speaking of our mothers. Rose said her mother had been gone these eight years and I inferred that she should be grateful she'd had her sister."

His mother's lips parted. "Oh. And you wonder why she was angry?"

Oliver shook his head. "There is something more, mother. More than her sister marrying the duke."

His mother lowered the sampler slightly and looked up at Oliver. "Perhaps you are right. She may have more she is hiding. But I believe there is kindness within her. You have seen it and so have I. Perhaps she needs someone to help her bring the good out."

Oliver's brow crinkled. "But how do I do such a thing? Especially when I know not what is troubling her."

His mother had shifted her focus back to the rug in her hands. "You are clever, but more importantly, you are kind, Oliver. Continue on the path you began, and I believe you will get the lady you desire in the end."

Oliver cringed slightly. "You mean I should not have slighted her the flowers? I did not know what to say with them. The only ones suitable seemed to be the purple carnations."

The dowager's head tipped to the side and she narrowed her eyes at him.

He ran a hand across the back of his neck. "She does not understand them anyhow."

His mother nodded. "But she *does* understand what it means not to get them."

Oliver's stomach churned. His mother always knew how to say exactly what he needed to hear.

"I will remedy this, mother."

She smiled at her needlework. "I know you will, dear."

* * *

ROSE PULLED a shawl across her shoulders and Oliver noticed the delicate curve of her neck. While she had agreed to go out tonight with Hannah and him, her excitement had not been piqued.

She had been in high dudgeons on and off for several days, but since his slight with the flowers that morning, she had seemed even more so. Why had he been so determined to show her he was displeased with her? Had it helped matters any? Quite the contrary.

They settled in the carriage and set off.

"Rose, are you not excited? Thank you for agreeing to let me come, Ollie. I know I was not a part of your original plans."

Oliver smiled at his sister, but it did not escape his notice that Rose did not answer the question. "Have you ever been to a circus, Rose?"

She glanced up and shook her head slightly. "Is that where we are to spend the evening?"

Oliver grinned. "Astley's Amphitheater is quite famous."

Rose barely turned toward him, but when she offered no conversation, Hannah took it up instead. "Oh, they have a ring in which horses run at high speeds while people do amazing tricks atop them. But there is also a stage where they will do a play for the second half. It is as if we are going to the theater and the menagerie at the same time!"

At least someone was excited. Rose neither smiled nor

frowned. It was as if there was no emotion left in her. She just nodded her head. "It sounds delightful."

From her response, one might guess they were going to watch a field being plowed rather than such a spectacle as Astley's.

Oliver ran a hand down his face. This woman was as vexing as anything he had ever encountered. But his mother's words rang through his mind and he sighed. For better or worse, she was his wife and they were shackled together until death took one of them. But he could not have this be the rest of his life. They had to find some sort of pleasant, if not truly happy, middle ground. Oliver thought on the wager he had placed and silently cursed himself.

The carriage finally pulled to a complete stop, allowing them to exit after some time waiting in the line of carriages.

Once everyone was handed out, Oliver extended both of his arms out, one to his wife and one to Hannah. Hannah excitedly took it, but Rose was more tentative. He could barely feel the weight of her hand on his arm, so lightly she set it there. It was as if she only wanted the illusion of contact, but did not desire to actually touch him.

He walked them in, much happier with their seats here than he had been at Sadler's Wells. They were on the second tier in a box almost directly across from the stage. It had taken some work and some words from the Duke of Shearsby to secure the seats, but Oliver hoped it would be worth it. It was his one chance, for he could not afford such extravagances often, to show his wife that life with a baron would not be as horrible as she thought.

Perhaps he was just trying to show people they were wrong about his marriage to Rose. Both were likely true. They could be happy together...or at least he hoped they could.

As the show began, Rose watched with very little enthusiasm. But as the horses and the tricks began, her eyes brightened. When the clowns teased the dancers and the horses, jumping out of the way just before being trampled or run down, the crowd laughed uproariously.

Oliver watched Rose from the corner of his eyes. He was fascinated as he watched her eyes widen right before the clown rolled out of the way. Or grin when the same clown scolded the horse for nearly running him down. She tilted her head to the side, studying the dancer as he rode the horse while standing on his hands.

When the performers stopped the show to reset the stage, she looked over at him and her smile faltered.

He tried not to let her reaction do the same to him. Smiling wider than was necessary, Oliver asked, "What do you think? Are you enjoying the performance?"

A small smile turned the corners of her mouth. Oliver wasn't sure if it was in response to his smile or the bouncing of Hannah in the next seat.

She nodded her head. "Very much. I had no idea such performances were to be found. It is all so very fantastic."

Hannah squeezed Rose's arm. "It is." She leaned over Rose and patted Oliver's arm. "Thank you, again, for allowing me to join you."

Oliver could not help but laugh. "Hannah, I will miss your enthusiasm come the Season after next."

Hannah sobered. "Whatever do you mean?"

Rose patted Hannah on the knee. "He means once you are presented and have come out, you will be expected to maintain a certain decorum."

Hannah slumped down in her seat. "You mean I shall have to become dull."

Rose looked on Hannah with her mouth hanging slightly open. She put her hand over her heart. "Miss Brandon, are you suggesting I am dull?"

Oliver laughed at Hannah's wide, apologetic eyes. "Oh,

certainly not, Rose. But I know you do not care what the *ton* thinks of you."

Rose stiffened next to Oliver and her mouth snapped shut. He reached for her hand, placing it on top of his arm and giving it a gentle squeeze before he released it. Leaning over, he whispered, "She meant it as a compliment."

Rose nodded. "I know. But...." Her quiet tones trailed off.

"It still hurts. I'm sorry I hurt you when I did not bring you flowers this morning."

Rose shrugged as if she cared not about it and Oliver's chest tightened. "It is no mind. My room looks like a hothouse already." Her words and expressions told two different stories.

His mother had been correct; she may not know what each flower he sent her symbolized, but she knew what he was telling her when he neglected to send her any.

"It was unkind of me and I want you to know I am sorry." The words seemed so inadequate.

She looked into his eyes and her breath came out stuttered and shallow. "I deserved your disdain." She turned toward the front, looking at the stage crowded with people setting up the next scene of the show. "What I said was awful. I used to be kind. I am not sure when or completely why I changed. I am sorry you were not able to marry that lady, the one I used to be." Her voice hitched and she withdrew her hand, twisting her fingers in her lap.

Oliver snatched her hand back, but this time he placed it on his hand.

The crowd shuffled to their seats as the show was set to begin again. Neither Oliver nor Rose said any more, both looking straight ahead. But Oliver thought of nothing that was happening on stage. All he could think about was the woman at his side. What had changed? He did know she could be kind. He had seen it with Hannah and even, at times, with him.

126

As the show began, Oliver swallowed hard as he gently and slowly moved his hand, turning his palm upward. He felt Rose lift her arm and he thought she might pull it away again. But instead it hovered above while he made the change of positions. When his arm was in place, she softly dropped her hand.

Without a word, Oliver pulled her hand down, so it was now resting in his palm. He curled his fingers up, intertwining them with hers. He glanced over when he heard her breath catch.

He had gone too far, pressed her for too much. Surely, she would take her hand back and keep it from his reach.

But she didn't. Instead she curled her fingers also, squeezing his hand just enough for him to know she did it on purpose.

Oliver sat staring at the stage with absolutely no idea what was happening. His wife was holding his hand and he felt there may actually be hope for them.

CHAPTER 15

Rose sat at her dressing table staring into the mirror, seeing nothing of her reflection, only Oliver's hand as it curled into her own. Just thinking on it sent her pulse racing.

He had apologized for not bringing her flowers this morning, but she had not imagined he would do something so intimate only moments afterward.

Rose closed her eyes. She had liked it. His hands were warm and strong. When he had rubbed his thumb along her index finger, she could think of nothing else. Had she not studied her history and already known the outcome of the Battle of Aboukir, Rose would have had no idea how the stage show ended, so distracted she was.

The door from her dressing room opened and Mary came into the room. "Ah, my lady. Did you have a pleasant evening?"

Rose felt her cheeks heat, as if she had been caught doing something untoward. "I did." She turned partially in her chair and looked up at her maid. "Mary, have you ever heard of Astley's? It was quite spectacular." At the shake of Mary's head, Rose spent the next several minutes describing everything from the first half of the show. She left out the second half, only because she had paid little attention, and she did not wish to share what she *had* been paying attention to during that time.

Rose removed the amethyst broach from her dress and went to place it in her jewelry box. Mary dropped the pins she was removing from Rose's hair and moved to Rose's side. "Let me put that away for you."

Rose waved her aside. "My box is right here, Mary. You finish removing my pins. I can see to my broach."

Mary slowly walked behind Rose, setting back to work on her hair. Her gaze flicked nervously from Rose's hands to the jewelry box.

Rose reached forward and opened the lower drawer in the box. She set the broach on the velvet lined tray and moved to push it closed but she stopped. The bag with her mother's pearls was not there. Rose opened the other drawer and lifted the top, her heart picking up its pace with each unsuccessful attempt to locate the bag.

She whipped around, feeling her hair pull from Mary's hands. "Mary, where are my mother's pearls? Have you seen them?"

Mary shook her head. "Not in a few days, my lady. I thought perhaps you had taken them to be fixed."

Rose watched Mary in the mirror. The girl would not raise her eyes. Perhaps it was because she was intent on her duties, but something felt amiss with her. "Mary, are you sure you do not know their whereabouts?"

Mary shook her head, but still her eyes stayed lowered. "I have no notion, my lady."

Rose closed the lid of the box with a shaking hand. It was bad enough she had never recovered the five pearls she had lost at the theater, but now to have them all missing? It was her one treasure from her mother.

Rose rubbed at her eyes with her fisted hand. The excitement from the evening faded with this new discovery.

Mary finished plaiting Roses hair and helped her slip into her night dress.

Rose climbed into bed. "You can finish straightening up in the morning, Mary. I wish to go to sleep now."

She blew out her candle before Mary had even made it into the dressing room.

Rose stared at the ceiling, thinking. Mary had grown up with Rose and Violet. Mary's mother, Jones, had served Rose's mother as a lady's maid. When Rose's mother had died, Jones had stayed on to serve Rose and Violet. It had only been natural, when Jones was unable to continue in their service, for Mary to take over for her mother. She had been training to be a lady's maid all her life. Rose and Violet knew they should have started calling Mary, *Jones,* as they had her mother, but they had never been able to make that change.

Rose rubbed at her temples trying to sooth the headache forming at the back of her eyes.

She had never thought Mary would steal from her. But the oddity of Mary's behavior—the averted eyes and guilty looks—made Rose wonder if she had been wrong about her maid.

Perhaps she should ask Violet's opinion.

ROSE ENTERED the breakfast room the next morning with a heavy heart. The more she thought on it, the more she was convinced of Mary's guilt. She could not come up with any other explanation.

Her mood lightened when she saw a large bouquet of

flowers sitting in her normal spot at the table. Daffodils inter-mixed with red and yellow tulips. A quiet squeal of delight sounded from Rose's lips as she raced around the table to smell them.

A small note was tucked inside, between a red and yellow tulip.

Rose- I enjoyed our evening together more than you could know. I look forward to many more such nights. Yours, O

It was the most intimate note he had written her to date. It was not flowery words of love, but it would certainly do.

She palmed the note, holding her hands to her chest. A warmth spread out, warming her from head to toe. Rose paused. Did Violet feel like this when she thought of the duke? The thought disquieted Rose. Oliver had mentioned the duke and Violet clearly had a love match. Rose had never doubted the duke loved her sister, but she had worked hard to convince herself that Violet did not share the duke's feelings. But what if that was not the case?

Rose tucked the note into the sleeve of her dress and moved to the sideboard to fill her plate with eggs, fried ham and toasted bread. As she buttered her scone, Rose continued to think on the notion that Violet may have similar feelings for her husband.

Violet had said she loved the duke, but Rose would have said such things also, if that would have insured he marry her. If she did actually love him, did it make a difference? Did it make what she did to Rose less horrific?

Rose frowned. She could not excuse what her sister had done, but it was giving Rose something to think on.

Oliver walked into the breakfast room. "Good morning, Rose. I hope you slept well."

Rose ducked her head. Why was she suddenly feeling shy? Something had changed last night. She frowned slightly. Had she not thought that before? And then things went wrong shortly thereafter?

"I did, thank you." She put a forkful of ham into her mouth, chewing for a moment. She swallowed and smiled. "And you?"

Oliver put his plate down next to hers. "I hope we are not standing on formalities today."

Rose shook her head.

He pulled out the chair and sat down next to her. "I slept exceptionally well. Better than I have in weeks."

His sleeve brushed her arm and gooseflesh broke out all over her skin. It was only his jacket, she chided herself.

The dowager came in, with Hannah trailing in behind her. "Ah, Lady Munsford. I did not expect to see you up so early after your late night."

Rose stopped her. "I wish you would call me Rose, my lady." She bit the inside of her cheek. Why was she so nervous about what the dowager would say? Would it be disastrous if she declined?

The dowager paused. "I should like that very much. Perhaps, seeing as your own good mother is no longer with us, you could call me Mother Brandon, or perhaps just Mama?"

Rose stared, her arms and legs feeling tingly. Could she be in earnest? It had been such a long time since she had uttered that name to someone.

"Never you mind, dear. My lady, is also acceptable."

Rose shook her head. "No. I did not pause because I found your suggestion distasteful. I am humbled by it." She took a deep breath. "Unless you have changed your mind, I should like to call you Mama." Rose liked the feel of the name on her lips.

The dowager nodded. "Then it is settled." Her eyes drifted to the flowers in the vase in front of Rose and her eyebrows rose high on her forehead. "What lovely flowers. Are they from Oliver?"

Rose smiled and glanced at her husband, nodding. "Yes." Rose gently fingered the petal of a red tulip. "Most people assume my favorite flower is the rose. But in truth, it is tulips I love most." Again, a shyness settled over her and she found she could not look at Oliver.

"I admit to having assumed that very thing. I shall try to remember it in the future." The dowager gave her son an odd look.

Rose glanced sideways at him and noticed he ducked his head, avoiding his mother's pointed look.

Hannah sat across the table from them. "I love tulips also." She picked up her fork. "Oliver always gives me yellow tulips because they symbolize—" Oliver cleared his throat loudly.

Hannah looked over at him with a furrowed brow. "What is it, Oliver? Are you not well?"

He pushed his nearly full plate away and pushed back from the table. "I am well, Hannah. I have just had my fill."

He looked almost pleadingly at Rose. "Would you care for a turn about the garden? I have to meet with my solicitor in an hour, but I thought a walk might be nice before I am sequestered indoors for the remainder of the day."

Rose popped one last bite into her mouth and nodded. "Yes. I should enjoy a turn. I believe I shall visit my sister later today."

He helped her with her chair and lead her toward the doorway. "Mother. Hannah." He dipped his head to them before they moved out of the room and into the corridor. He motioned toward the entry way. "Do you need your bonnet?"

Rose nodded her head. "The garden is shady this time of day, but I believe I will leave directly after our walk for Heatherton House."

They fetched hats and gloves and moved toward the back of the house, Rose tying her ribbons as they walked.

Oliver was quiet for a moment. "You have not visited your

sister once since we married. I thought perhaps you did not wish to see her."

Rose cringed at his obvious attempt to speak of Violet without earning an angry outburst from her again.

"You need not skirt the subject of my sister, Oliver. I promise I will keep my foul temper in check."

He pushed the door to the terrace open and stepped through before holding out his hand to help her down the small step. Rose was happy when he did not release her hand, instead intertwining his fingers with hers. "I do not wish to cause you distress, that is all."

Rose nodded. "I have a concern and I wished to get Violet's opinion on it."

Oliver pulled her hand from his and tucked it into the crook of his arm, bringing her closer to him. "If you should need a man's opinion, I am at your service."

Rose chuckled. "I appreciate your willingness. It has to do with Mary. I am concerned she may have stolen my mother's pearls." Oliver stiffened and Rose paused. She looked up at him. He must still be feeling the guilt of his role in breaking the necklace. "I wish to get Violet's opinion on the matter. I would never have thought it of Mary, but I can come to no other conclusion."

Oliver's voice came out strained. "But I thought Mary had been with you for the whole of her life. Do you not know her character well enough to know the answer?"

Rose nodded. "I thought I did. But when I discovered my bag missing after the theater last night, I asked Mary about it. She acted very odd."

Oliver stopped walking. "My dear, I just remembered I was to ready some papers before my solicitor arrives. May we resume this walk tomorrow perhaps?"

Rose nodded, not certain what to say.

He turned and followed the path back to the house.

Rose frowned, turning in the opposite direction of her husband, instead following the path around to the gate at the far side of the grounds.

She walked down the small alleyway running between two rows of houses. Rose came out on the street, walking several rods and turning the corner, she saw their carriage in front of the house.

When the footman saw her coming, he hopped down from the carriage, opened the door and handed her up. "Thank you, Francis."

It was not a long drive to Grosvenor Square and Heatherton House, but it was long enough to allow Rose a moment to think.

Oliver had acted just as oddly as Mary had when Rose had mentioned the pearls. What was it about the pearls that made people react so strangely?

The carriage stopped and Rose looked up at her sister's London home. It was one of the largest and finest houses in Grosvenor Square. It should have been hers. Rose swallowed down the jealousy that always seemed to surface when she looked up at the façade of Heatherton House.

Rose walked up the steps, rapping lightly on the door. Billings opened the door. "Lady Munsford. Her Grace has been expecting you."

She handed off her bonnet and gloves. The butler handed them to a nearby footman. "Please, follow me."

A small dog ran from a room on Rose's left into a room on her right, nearly tripping her. She shook her head. Janus was something she had not missed since being away.

Rose looked down the corridor. She had not been in Heatherton House since the morning of her wedding. It was strange to be back and treated as a guest.

Billings opened the door to the purple morning room. Had

Rose been permitted to find her sister without assistance, this would have been the first place she would have looked. She knew it to be Violet's favorite room.

Violet was seated in a chair by a window overlooking the back gardens. She looked up when Rose entered.

Violet smiled, but Rose could see it was guarded and forced. They had not parted on the friendliest of terms. Violet stood and walked toward Rose, her hands stretched out.

Rose allowed her sister to take her hands and was surprised she did not feel as angry as was her usual. What had changed?

Rose smiled. *Oliver.*

"I was so pleased to get your note this morning." Violet sounded as she always did. Cheerful and happy, if a little hesitant.

"I am sorry I am imposing on you at such an early hour, but I needed to get your opinion on a most concerning matter."

Violet led her to a settee and motioned for them to sit down.

"Tell me, what is bothering you? Is it Lord Munsford?" There was a touch of concern in Violet's creased brow.

How could Violet feel concern for Rose? After everything? Rose's stomach burned. She had not felt concern for Violet, even after she learned of Mr. McPhail's cruelty toward her. Rose looked at her hands. How had she become so wicked? She focused her attention on the button at her wrist. "Mother's pearls have gone missing. When I questioned Mary and asked if she had seen them, she acted quite strangely. Almost as if she were the one responsible."

Violet sat back. "Mary? Steal mother's pearls? I cannot imagine a situation in which she would do such a thing."

Rose nodded. "I agree. But I can come up with no other solution. Who else could have done it?"

"What of the other staff? They are new to you. Is there anyone you have seen acting suspiciously?"

Rose shook her head. "Only Mary. And my husband. But I think he was only feeling guilty for breaking the necklace in the first place."

Violet raised a brow. "He broke your necklace?"

"It was an accident. He was trying to move me away from some ruffians and did not notice my hand was on the necklace." Rose smiled. "He was very sorry. I received a very pretty bouquet the morning after."

Now both of Violet's brows rose high on her head. "Tell me, Rose. How is his lordship?"

Rose's face heated and she knew she was coloring up. "He is well. He is meeting with his solicitor today." She knew that was not what Violet was after, but Rose did not know what or how much she wished to share.

"He gave you flowers? That is very gentlemanly of him."

Rose smiled. She could count on one hand how many times the duke had given Violet flowers. "Yes. He gives me a new bouquet every morning. Today it was daffodils with red and yellow tulips."

Violet grinned. "He knows your favorite flower."

Rose nodded. This was nice. As much as she had grown to love Hannah, this was different. Violet was a married woman. Additionally, they had shared many of the same experiences in their youth. Suddenly, Rose felt the loss of her sister. "Last night he took me to Astley's Amphitheater. It was delightful." Rose looked pointedly at Violet. "Have you been?"

Violet shook her head. "No. But if you recommend it, I shall have Tad secure us seats." Violet sat back against the cushions, appearing more relaxed than she had since Rose arrived. "I should rather have been with you last night than Lord Grafton's dinner party."

Rose's smile dropped. "Lord Grafton? The Marquess?"

Violet nodded. "Your evening sounds far more diverting."

Violet had spent the evening with Lord Grafton and who knows what other nobility while Rose had been watching a silly animal show. Why had she even come here? Just so Violet could gloat about how much better her life was than Rose's?

Rose stood up. "I need to be going. I promised Hannah we could go to the Egyptian Exhibit at the museum." It wasn't true, but Rose didn't care. She needed to leave, and any excuse would do.

Violet stood, obviously sensing the change in Rose. The guarded smile once again slid into place on Violet's face. "Thank you for visiting. I hope to see you again soon."

Rose walked quickly from the room, nearly snatching her bonnet and gloves away from Billings.

Francis helped her into the carriage, and she collapsed against the back. She had nearly believed she could forgive Violet for destroying her life. But she couldn't. Violet was leading the life meant for Rose, attending her parties and associating with her friends. Rose just could not let her off the hook so easily.

CHAPTER 16

The front door opened, and Oliver felt his heart skip. Rose was back from her sister's.

Several minutes later, a door slammed above him.

Oliver took a deep breath. He had been afraid the visit would end this way. What had the duchess said to Rose that made her so angry? Perhaps he should talk to the duke and demand he keep his wife in check.

Oliver looked over the paperwork Mr. Beaverton had left for him. He picked up another pile of bills, adding them to the stack. He rubbed his thumb and fingers over his eyes. How would he ever be able to recover from the debt his father had put them in? From the corner of his eyes, he spotted the small velvet bag, sitting in the corner of his desk drawer.

Guilt crawled up from his stomach, tightening his chest. He should have told her he knew it was not Mary, but he did not want to spoil her surprise. He had an appointment tomorrow afternoon with the jeweler. It should not take long to fix the necklace. She would have it back before long.

Another door slammed and Oliver pushed himself to standing. Was it possible he could help cheer her up? They had not finished their walk earlier. Perhaps that would help. She always seemed to enjoy the gardens. He made his way out of his study and up to the next floor. A maid scurried down the corridor away from his wife's chambers.

Oliver stood in front of the door and took a deep breath. He squared his shoulders and knocked quickly.

"Enter." The tone was clipped.

He pushed open the door. Rose sat in the chair by the window. She looked up when the door swung open. He thought he saw her face brighten when she saw him, but that could have been his imagination.

She tossed aside the book she was reading. "I thought you were to be meeting with your solicitor for the whole of the day." She didn't sound as angry as the last time, but there was obvious frustration. Oliver congratulated himself on learning this much about his wife.

"I thought we were to go over the papers together, but he had other appointments, so he just left them for me to go over alone. We will discuss them next week."

"Hmmm." She turned fully toward him in her chair. "Do you need my help?"

Oliver smiled, glad she was comfortable enough with their relationship to ask. "Perhaps." Oliver bounced on the balls of his feet a few times, his hand clasped behind his back. "But first I thought we could continue our walk. I suddenly have the entire afternoon available."

She tilted her head to the side and her face softened. There was still a look in her eyes he did not understand. "I would like that. But are you not frightened of me?"

Oliver laughed. "What? You have never frightened me."

"Penny, the maid cannot boast as much." She took a long breath. "Let me fetch my bonnet and we can go. Are we to stroll in our garden or did you have somewhere else in mind?"

Oliver flipped open his pocket watch. "It is the fashionable hour, but I am not opposed to it if you aren't."

Rose swallowed. "Hyde Park, then?"

"Unless you do not wish to go. But I find I would like the *ton* to see my beautiful wife walking on my arm in Hyde Park." Oliver secretly prayed no one would say anything unkind to her today. Perhaps, after breakfast and the flowers, she could have managed what the society might banter at her. But this afternoon, he was not sure what would happen.

"Hyde Park it is." She gracefully rose from her chair and walked over to him.

When she came up beside him, he took her hand in his and without knowing why, leaned down and pressed a kiss to her temple. This was right. "That's my girl. Hannah was right, you know. You don't need to care what the *ton* has to say. We know the truth."

He thought his words would help to give her strength, but she only seemed to sag a bit more.

HYDE PARK WAS BUSTLING with both man and beast. The promenade was almost elbow to elbow with people. Oliver pulled Rose close to him, placing her hand between his body and his arm, her fingers clutching at him.

He placed his free arm around her waist, guiding her through the crowd.

Oliver spotted Miss Carlyle and Lord Kent coming toward

them on the other side of the path. He felt when Rose saw them, too.

As they were about to pass, Oliver saw Miss Carlyle open her mouth, her green eyes narrowing in on Rose.

Before a word could be spoken, Oliver veered Rose to the right, taking the path which led to Kensington Gardens. As they crossed over the ha-has separating the garden from Hyde Park, the crowds thinned out and he heard Rose breathe deeply.

"Thank you."

"You have no need to thank me, my dear." Oliver was happy when, instead of pulling away from him now that they were away from the heaviest of the crowds, she leaned in closer and rested her head on his arm.

Once in Kensington Gardens, they stepped off the path, instead walking along the banks of the Long Water. Many couples rowed small boats through the water. "Would you care to rent a boat? We could go back to Hyde Park and row the Serpentine until it connects here with Long Water."

Rose shook her head. "I am content as we are."

"Rose, what do you enjoy doing?"

She lifted her head and looked at him. "I don't understand your meaning."

"I have seen you stitch, and it seems only to frustrate you. You play the piano, but only when I have asked. Do you enjoy painting or drawing? What is it you love to do?"

Rose shrugged. " I am proficient in most things, as a lady ought to be. But those pursuits are not how I prefer to spend my time."

"Do you like to read?"

Rose shrugged. "If I must."

"What of art? You did not mention if you paint or draw." Oliver did not know why he cared, but he found he very much wanted to find something she enjoyed. Perhaps if she had something she loved, it would help her release those things she did not. At the least, maybe it would make her happy for a time.

"I have done a few silhouettes, but that is all. I have never tried oils or even sketching with charcoal." Her brow furrowed. "Although, I do not know why I have not."

Oliver smiled. "Very good."

Rose sighed.

Oliver glanced over at her and saw her eyes flutter shut briefly. "Are you tired? We can return if you desire."

"No. I am just enjoying the weather. I needed this today."

"I noticed you were unhappy when you returned from your sister's visit." Did he not learn from the last time? He knew from experience that mentioning the duchess never brought pleasant conversations. Yet here he was, opening his mouth like a dolt looking for an argument. But now that he had started the conversation, he found he wanted to know more. How could he help if he did not know the problem? "Did it not go well?"

Rose sighed again. This one less contented. "It started out well enough. She agrees with you that there must be another explanation about the pearls."

Oliver grunted low in his throat. This was not the conversation he wanted to have again.

"Then I told her of the flowers you have given me." A soft smile played at her lips. She had such lovely lips.

"The duke does not give Violet flowers every day of their marriage."

He was glad she had chosen to ignore the one day he had not given them to her.

"Does that make me the better husband? I should like to be able to inform His Grace of his deficiencies when next we meet."

Rose giggled and for a moment she reminded him of Hannah. Had he ever heard Rose giggle before? It was delightful.

"For my money, yes. You are the better husband." Oliver's chest puffed out slightly. He did not realize how badly he had wanted her to say yes. By agreeing that he was the better husband, did that mean she no longer regretted marrying him instead of the duke?

"I am glad to hear it." Oliver's voice came out softer than he had anticipated. "The visit seems to have been quite pleasant."

Rose stopped. "Violet mentioned that they had spent last evening at Lord Grafton's party. It is one of the most sought-after invitations and we were not invited. She reminded me of how far I have fallen." She looked up at him. "And I have taken you with me."

"I will speak to the duke and ask him to speak to his wife. She should not intentionally upset you."

They began walking again and Rose shook her head adamantly. "No." She nearly shouted. Several people in boats on the water turned in their direction. "that is to say, please do not bother yourself."

"It is no bother if it means your happiness."

Rose pointed to a bench in a copse of trees in the distance. "Do you mind if we sit there? There is something you should know about Violet and me."

Oliver nodded and led her toward the bench, helping her to sit before taking a seat next to her. Why did she wish to sit in order to tell him something? With the way she was sitting, he could only see her face in profile.

She lifted her hand to her throat, but then dropped it. Instead, she ran her hands down the front of her skirt a few times. Her hands shook slightly. "How much do you know about my situation?"

She still faced straight ahead, as if she were talking to the Long Water, not him.

"I know you were engaged to the Duke of Shearsby, an

arrangement made between his uncle and your father." Rose nodded.

"Once you arrived at Morley Park, he threw you over in favor of your sister, neither of them caring about the repercussions." It was the one aspect of the duke, Oliver found difficult to reconcile with the man he knew.

Rose swallowed. "That is only part of the story. The part I knew could not be hidden from society. Everyone would reason out what had happened when the duke came to London with Violet on his arm."

Why would she not look at him?

"The story starts even before we arrived at Morley Park. Violet met the duke not far from our house in Cheshire. He came upon her after she had been harmed by a man from our neighborhood, a Mr. McPhail. He and Violet had been close while they grew up, but then he joined the army. He was away for years and had just returned." Rose took a breath and glanced over at him. "Violet never told me about seeing him. I learned of it much later."

She sighed deeply. "When Violet met the duke the first time, she did not know his name or who he was, he was just a man who found her and saw that she returned home safely. Then, oddly enough, on our way to Morley, we came upon some trouble and two gentlemen rescued us. We learned later one of the gentlemen was the duke. It was the second time Violet had met this man and still she did not know who he was. I believe she had already formed an attachment to him by this time. I did not see it. But when I look back on it now, it was there."

"It was not until we reached Morley Park that we learned the duke and his friend were the men who had saved us. For me it was a cleaver story I could tell my friends when we came to London after our marriage."

Oliver stretched out on the bench, kicking his legs out in front of him and crossing his ankles. He did not know why she was telling him this story. It was more detailed than he had previously heard, but it didn't seem to change what happened.

"You know what happened then. The more time we spent at Morley Park, the more I could see the duke developing an attachment to Violet. I tried to turn his affections toward me, but only succeeded in pushing him more toward her, until he severed the engagement and asked my father for Violet's hand."

Oliver nodded. "Yes, just as I said." He moved to stand up, but Rose put her hand out to stop him.

"What you don't know—few do because my sister and the duke have kept it secret—is what happened next. I overheard the duke ask my father for Violet's hand. I was so angry with her." Rose closed her eyes, her teeth clenched together. "She was my sister. She was supposed to be loyal to me. But instead she professed to love the man I was to marry. She took him and the title away from me."

Rose took a stuttering breath.

Oliver straightened in his seat and leaned forward. He did not know what Rose was about to tell him, but he could feel it was bad.

"Mr. McPhail, the one who harmed Violet before, convinced me to help him get Violet alone. He said if he could get her away from Morley Park, she would realize that she loved him and not the duke. I agreed."

Rose turned guilty eyes on Oliver. "Mr. McPhail told me she loved *him*. I was so mad at her. And how was I to know he was not telling the truth?" Her cheek twitched and Oliver reached up to rub it gently. Looking in her eyes he knew she had not believed the man. She had done it for herself; to get her sister out of the way, to get what she wanted.

Oliver swallowed and the words Rose spoke earlier came back

to him. *I used to be kind. I am not sure when or completely why I changed. I am sorry you were not able to marry the lady I was before.*

"I helped lure her into the orangery and Mr. McPhail took her to Gretna. I thought if she was gone and the duke thought she had left him for another, he would marry me instead. I thought Violet was just saying she loved the duke so he would marry her. I didn't believe she meant it."

Oliver toed at the grass in front of them. His stomach turned over when he thought of the duchess being carried away. "What happened to her?" Was that his voice? He barely recognized it.

"The duke went after her and saved her. It was then I realized how much he loved her, but it is only recently that I have come to realized she loves him just as much. She always has. When I came home from visiting her, I was angry with her for taking away an invitation to Lord Grafton's party. But deep down, when I am alone with my thoughts, I know she could have taken so much more had she allowed what I did to be exposed."

Oliver could feel her watching him.

"Had you known; you surely would never have married such a lady." Her voice hitched. It was not a question. She knew the answer, just as Oliver did. His chest hurt and he realized he had feelings for her. But she was right. He would never have married her had he known the truth.

But he *had not* known and now they *were* married. What were they to do now?

Oliver took a deep breath. "It was not your sister's fault we did not go to the Grafton's party. It was mine. We received an invitation and I declined it. I did not believe you were inclined to attend."

Oliver did not think Rose's face could look more ashen. He was wrong.

149

CHAPTER 17

Would anyone notice if I stayed in here forever?

Rose looked up at the ceiling above her bed. She flopped her arm over her eyes, hoping that by blocking the light she might lessen the pounding in her head.

Her eyes burned, a result of her mostly sleepless night.

Why had she told Oliver what she had done? She believed he was starting to care for her. But she had put an end to that yesterday. He may not divorce her—his reputation would surely suffer if he did, though hers would be completely destroyed—but that did not stand to reason he would ever live in the same house, or even the same county as her.

Her chest squeezed. Would he send her away immediately or wait until the Season was over? She pulled a pillow on top of her head and snuggled the rest of her body down in the covers. She should probably get up and call Mary to help her pack, but she could not face the task just now.

A knock sounded at her door, but Rose ignored it. Why could they not leave her alone? It was probably Hannah. Happy

Hannah. Gah! Rose did not want to see happy when she was so miserable.

The knocking stopped and Rose shut her eyes, trying to block out her thoughts.

Rose stirred when Mary came into the room. "It's time to get up, Lady Munsford."

Lady Munsford. Every day when someone called her name, Rose would be forced to remember what she could not have.

"A maid asked me to bring these flowers in to you. She said she knocked, but you must have still been abed."

Rose slowly pulled the pillow off her head. Flowers? Surely, he did not send her flowers after what she had told him. He had not even been able to speak to her for the ride back to their townhouse yesterday. And he had been absent for dinner, not even telling his mother or Hannah where he had gone.

Pushing herself up onto her elbows, Rose looked to where Mary placed the flowers in an empty space on the window ledge. Several stems of purple hyacinths filled the vase, with green ivy spilling down the sides.

"Please fetch me the note, Mary."

Mary pulled the paper wedged between two of the blooms and brought it over, placing it in Rose's upturned hand.

Rose opened the single folded sheet.

Because we both need to forgive.

Yours, O

She folded the paper back up, her nostrils flaring slightly. Who did he think he was to tell her she needed to forgive?

Rose dropped back down onto the pillow, opening the note and reading it again. Taking a slow deep breath, she forced her anger to leave her. What good had it done her up to now?

He was right. Rose did need to forgive Violet. Did the flowers mean he forgave Rose? Truly forgave her? How was it so easy for him to do so?

Rose stared up at the ceiling. The vicar from her parish church in Kidsgrove spoke often on forgiveness. He said one needed to ask to be forgiven before full forgiveness was possible. He was probably not envisioning the kind of forgiveness Rose sought.

Her heart hammered in her chest at the thought of asking Violet to forgive her. Would she be able to?

Mary walked in from the dressing room carrying a morning dress and slippers.

"Are you ready to dress, my lady?"

Rose threw back the overs and slid her legs over the side of the bed. She pushed herself to standing and trudged over to the dressing table where Mary began to separate the plait down her back.

The girl was quiet as she worked, which was fine for Rose. Her head hurt and she was not up to idle chatter today.

Mary glanced at Rose's reflection. "Your eyes look puffy this morning. Did you not sleep well?"

Rose gently shook her head so as not to interfere with Mary's work.

"Breakfast has already been cleared. But I saved you a plate. I can bring some cucumbers when I bring up your tray and you can put them on your eyes. It should help take the puffiness down."

Rose leaned closer, looking at her offending eyes. Besides being puffy, dark circles sat beneath. Her face looked drawn and worn.

"Yes, Mary. That would be most helpful."

Mary made a few more twists, pinning them in place on Rose's head. Her face may look a disaster, but at least her hair was pretty.

"Before you bring up my tray, I would like to go and thank Lord Munsford for the flowers."

Rose stood up and followed Mary to the chair where her dress was draped. She lifted her arms as Mary pulled off her night dress.

"If you wish to see the master before he leaves, you will want to hurry. I heard his valet saying he would be leaving soon and would be away for most of the day."

Rose impatiently dropped her arms as Mary gently pulled the dress down around her body. "Make quick work, Mary. I do not want to miss him."

Mary's fingers fumbled on several buttons as she hurriedly tried to secure them down Rose's back. When the sash was tied, Mary gave Rose a slight pat on the back.

"Hurry, now, my lady."

Rose rushed out of her room and down the stairs, nearly knocking Oliver to the floor when she ran into him on the landing. He looked up and smiled, though Rose could see it did not reach all the way to his eyes. "You are up. I had thought I may not see you before I left this morning." Was he hoping that to be the case? Was he disappointed he must see her now? Rose tried not to let her vulnerability show.

"I was coming to see you. Mary said you were to be gone the remainder of the day."

He lifted a hand toward her, motioning for her to go first.

"I wished to thank you for the beautiful flowers. I believe you are correct. I shall visit Violet today."

His body relaxed slightly. Was he glad she was going to apologize to Violet? For the stiltedness in his tone, she questioned how much he truly forgave her. But it was no matter; she knew what she had to do concerning her sister. Truthfully, she had known for some time but had not allowed herself to accept it. She was doing it for herself, not her husband.

"I am glad for you and the duchess." He tapped the newspaper he was holding against his open palm.

Rose nodded, unsure what was left to say. She gave one final hard nod and turned toward the stairs.

"Oh, Rose?"

She turned back. Would he ask her to accompany him wherever he was going?

"The post came this morning. You received a letter from your father."

Rose perked up. It was not what she had been hoping for, but still a letter from her father was a welcome surprise.

"It is on my desk in the study—" he paused and looked at his pocket watch. His brow furrowed. "I could fetch it for you, but I must see my mother first." There was hesitation in his voice.

Rose waved a hand in the air. "I can get it. You go on to your mother."

A relieved look crossed his face and he gave her a quick smile before he turned and walked down the stairs.

Rose watched him until he stepped onto the wood floor of the entryway. He turned and saw her staring at him. Again, he flashed a quick, but not complete smile.

Rose sighed and turned toward the corridor, intent on retrieving her father's letter so she could read it as she ate.

She pushed the door to Oliver's study open and stepped inside. The curtains were partially closed, casting much of the room in shadow. Only the curtain to the right of the desk remained fully open. She moved to the window and threw open the remaining curtains, filling the room with light.

Rose walked around the room, running her fingers over the worn leather on a highbacked chair. She took in a deep breath. The room smelled of her husband, like lime and mint. Just breathing in the scent settled her nerves and mind. She felt safe here. She continued to study the room, reading the spines of the books lining the shelves. Were these books of his choosing? The ones he read for entertainment and learning? Books on philosophy, mythology and government mingled with novels on the shelves. But the books on horticultural and garden planning were at eye level and were obviously well used. Rose smiled. She would never be able to look on a plant or flower without thinking on Oliver.

Rose pulled a few books from the shelf, thumbing through their contents. Most of the words meant nothing to her, but the pictures were beautiful and of such quality she could easily see them hanging in a frame on the wall.

Clutching it to her chest, she closed her eyes. A noise from the corridor jerked her eyes open and she fumbled the book back onto the shelf. Her eyes darted about the room.

Quickly she moved behind the desk, looking for the letter addressed to her.

It was not obviously visible on the desktop. Rose lifted the corner of a stack of papers. Several notices of payment slipped from the stack. Her eyes bulged at the amounts listed at the bottom of each notice. She had known they were in financial trouble, but this was more than she suspected. Her hands shook as she placed the bills back in the stack. What if someone caught her? Rose finally found a small stack of letters sticking out from beneath a ledger book. Rose picked up the book, sifting through the letters until she found the one from her father. Letting the ledger fall back onto the desk, she turned to leave, but stopped.

Clutching the letter in both hands to her chest, her gaze dropped back to the ledger. Perhaps she had only seen the worst of the bills. The ledger would give a more accurate accounting.

She reached a hand forward, pulling it back once. What was she doing? This was not her concern. Rose bit the inside of her cheek. Had he not said it was her money which would be used to save the family? Did that not *make* this her concern?

Rose swallowed and flipped the book open to the page marked

with a silk ribbon. Her eyes moved down the pages, her brain taking a moment to interpret what was written.

She dropped into the chair behind his desk. Her dowry would not be enough to repay all the debt his father had incurred. It would likely take them years to clear it up, unless they came up with a plan. A very good plan. Rose dropped her letter back onto the desk and rested her face in her hands, rubbing at her eyes with her palms.

She slowly pulled her hands off and caught a glimpse of red in the small crack of the desk drawer. Rose focused on the drawer, sparing a quick glance toward the study door. What if there was a second ledger? What if they owed even more money? Did she dare look in that ledger also?

Licking her lips, she gently tugged the drawer open. But it was not a ledger she found tucked inside the drawer. It was her bag of pearls.

Rose lifted it up and her stomach dropped. She pulled the top of the bag open, hoping it was not the pearls inside. As several pearls dropped into her hand, her heart sank.

It appeared Oliver's flowers were not about forgiving her sister but rather preparing her to forgive him for stealing her pearls. Rose swallowed. Why had he not just asked her for the money? She would have let him take the money from her dowry, rather than lose her mother's necklace.

Rose took a stuttering breath. It did explain why he was being so nice to her and forgiving her for keeping her past a secret. He had secrets of his own.

The door moaned quietly, and Rose looked up guiltily. Oliver walked into his study. He smiled until his eyes landed on the red bag in her hands.

Rose stared at him. The expression on his face was all she needed to see. Why did the thought of him stealing the pearls make her want to cry? "It seems I was mistaken about Mary," Rose said, her voice dull. She stood up.

"I had hoped you would not find them."

Rose's eyes enlarged. "I am sure you did. Why did you not just ask me for the money?"

Oliver's brow creased. "What?"

She held up the bag. "You need not have taken them, Oliver. I would give you whatever money you need. I would have even asked the duke if it came to that."

He shook his head from side to side. "Rose. There is a misunderstanding. I did not steal your pearls. That is to say, I did not take them to pay off a debt. How could you think such a thing?"

Rose stared at him. If she told him what she found, he would be angry with her. But if they did not have trust, they really had nothing. She lifted the ledger. "You said I was shrewd. It did not take much to decipher this."

His face pinked. "I would never steal from you to pay for any of that."

"Then how do you explain these?" She shook the bag, the beads making a quiet noise.

Oliver walked to the desk and took the bag from her hand. "It was to be a surprise. That is the appointment I am off to. I am meeting with a jeweler to have your pearls restrung."

She tilted her head. Did she believe him? She stared at him, their gazes locking. Rose believed she knew her husband well enough to know he was telling her the truth. She came around the desk. "Really?"

His shoulders relaxed. "Yes, really."

Rose moved close to him, looking up into his face. "Thank you." She went up on her tip-toes and kissed him on the cheek.

He jerked away from her, as if her touch had burned him. "How could you believe I would do such a thing?"

He was right. How could she have thought such a thing? Did she not know him better than that? Rose looked at her fingers, rubbing each one until they were bleached white. "I am sorry, Oliver, for thinking you would betray me. I am trying to be better. Really, I am."

Oliver stood rooted in place.

Rose saw several emotions flit across his face.

She took a step back and he reached out a hand, grabbing her by the wrist. He gently pulled her to him, leaning down and brushing his lips against hers. "All is forgiven, my lady."

His lips were soft and the kiss was tender. Rose felt her knees weaken as his lips became more persistent. He pressed small kisses along her jaw and down her neck. She tilted her head to the side, allowing him more access.

A low moan sounded from his throat as he pulled her closer.

How could he forgive her so easily? Her earlier question floated through her mind once. Then it came again. By the third time, she had come more to her senses. Yes, how could he continually forgive her so easily?

Rose put her hands on his chest and pushed him away. He looked at her, passion and confusion warring for prominence in his gaze.

After learning what she had done, how could he want her? There had to be something amiss. He must be playing a role for some reason.

Rose shook her head. "No. This isn't right. Something isn't right."

She snatched up her father's letter off the desk and hurried from the room before he could stop her.

CHAPTER 18

Oliver paced back and forth in front of the jeweler's shop. He was early for his appointment, but he was still anxious that the man was not there yet. Even though Rose knew now that Oliver had the pearls and that Mary had not stolen them, he would feel more comfortable when they were back in her box, fully strung.

Oliver rubbed his hand across the back of his neck. His wife. She continued to baffle him. It seemed every time they made a stride forward, something happened to throw them back.

He frowned. His pride still stung, that she would believe him capable of stealing in order to pay off his debts. Oliver breathed deeply. But had he not married for just that reason? But marrying was different. He had made no pretense of love or admiration. She had known from the beginning the arrangement was for the money. Oliver scowled. The admission did not make him feel any better. Was that why she had pulled back from their kiss?

Rose had said she was trying. Trying to see the good in people before the bad. Did the kiss on the cheek she had given him, indicate the truthfulness of her statement? Oliver ran a hand through his hair. He had almost ruined the moment by letting his wounded pride get in the way.

Oliver licked his lips, almost tasting her lips again. He frowned when he thought back to the fear he had seen in her eyes as she pulled away. What was she afraid of? Was he reading more into their interactions than was really there?

Oliver wished he had been home to see her face when she saw the honeysuckle in her bouquet this morning. She would certainly suspect he had put it in because of what she had told him about her mother. But it was so much more to him than that, especially since that kiss.

A small man with a balding head strolled toward him. He swung a looking glass in one hand and a cane in the other. He stopped in front of the store and looked at Oliver. "Lord Munsford?"

Oliver nodded his head. "Yes. Thank you for meeting me, Mr. Stod."

The man nodded and turned toward the door of the store. He dropped the looking glass to dangle on its chain and withdrew a key from his waistcoat.

He opened the door and walked inside, pushing aside the curtains to let light in. Mr. Stod motioned Oliver over to a high counter at the far end of the shop. He picked up a candle and lit it off the coals banked in the fireplace. After he tended several other candles located around the store, light filled the small room.

He walked behind the counter and motioned Oliver forward. "May I see the pearls?"

Withdrawing the small bag from his pocket, Oliver sat it on the counter. He had been so looking forward to this meeting only a few hours ago. But now he was uncertain about so much. He ran a hand down his face.

Mr. Stod slowly shook the pearls out, corralling them into a small circle. He looked them over, hmming over each pearl he pick up. He used a large magnifying glass, holding several of the pearls under it to examine.

"These pearls are a very high quality. And each matched precisely in size."

Oliver nodded, because he was not sure what he was supposed to say. He knew nothing of gems.

"I can see why you are anxious to get them secured back on the string. It would be easy to lose one when they are loose as they are."

"Can you fix it?" Oliver heard the urgency in his voice.

Mr. Stod nodded. "Of course I can fix it." The man seemed affronted by the question. "I should not be a jeweler of any worth could I not fix something so simple."

Oliver gave an apologetic smile. "It can be done quickly?"

"You cannot rush excellence, sir. I can return it to you in three days' time."

A small grunt escaped Oliver's lips. He had hoped it would not take so long. In truth, after today, he did not know if his wife would still be speaking to him in three days' time.

Mr. Stod narrowed his eyes. "You find it unacceptable?" He scooped the pearls into his hand and dropped them back into the velvet bag. "You are welcome to seek out another jeweler."

Oliver sighed. "No. I have asked around and everyone I spoke with mentioned your preciseness. I was just hoping to give the necklace back to my wife sooner. It was meant to be a surprise..." Oliver trailed off. Rose had all but ruined the surprise this morning. But he and the duke had discussed attending Vauxhall, if they could ever get their wives on cordial terms. He hoped to have them back by that time, at least.

"Ah, surprising your wife. I shall work into the night and have them ready for you tomorrow next."

Oliver grinned. "Thank you, Mr. Stod. I am in your debt."

The jeweler smiled. "I, too, have a wife, my lord."

Oliver shook the man's hand and walked out of the shop. Shutting the door behind him, he let a large breath hiss through his teeth. It would not be the surprise he had hoped for, but perhaps there was still a thing or two Rose did not know.

* * *

OLIVER SAT at a table near the window in Gunter's, waiting for his mother and sister to join him.

He stared out the window, watching the ladies in their carriages under the shade of the trees lining Berkley Square, their escorts leaning against the railings nearby. Several servers darted across the street delivering the ices to the carriage occupants. Oliver cringed as one waiter narrowly missed the wheel of a passing carriage.

He sighed. He was not in the mood for such entertainments today. After discovering Rose in his study, he was out of sorts. Oliver felt his pocket for the coins. This was an extravagance he really could not afford, but he had promised Hannah—long before he learned of his father's ill-conceived investments—she could come to the famous shop when Oliver brought her to London. If Oliver did not order an ice, he had just enough money to buy one for his mother and one for Hannah.

The door swung open and Oliver heard Hannah's laughter before he saw her.

His mother had a hat box swinging from her arm. Oliver bristled. It was not like his mother to act so irresponsibly. She knew of their difficulties. Why was she out shopping for bonnets?

Lady Munsford stood, waiting for Oliver to help them with their chairs. Once seated, she placed her box on the floor beside her.

Oliver leaned forward. "Mother, what are you doing shopping for hats? I thought we had discussed this."

His mother patted his hand and smiled, meeting him halfway across the table. "It is an empty box, dear. But one must keep up appearances."

Oliver scooted back into his seat. "Oh? I am quite certain the whole of the *ton* knows of our ruination. I believe the box unnecessary."

The dowager shook her head. "The *ton* does not know the extent, dear. Ruination can mean different things to different people. No one need know how bad we truly have it."

Oliver shrugged. "Whatever you think is best, Mother. As long as you are not actually purchasing new bonnets."

A waiter approached and he ordered he two ices. His mother smiled. "Ices at Gunter's is a good idea. For no one who was truly ruined could afford such a luxury."

Oliver swallowed hard, running his finger over the table edge. What would his wife think if she knew they were here? While she had not said as much, Oliver was convinced it was the discovery of his substantial debt that had her pulling away from their kiss.

"How is your wife, son? I have not seen her much of late."

Oliver shrugged. What was he to say? I tried to kiss her and she ran away? Instead he settled on something more general. "I believe she is well, Mother. Or she seemed to be so when last I saw her." *Well* might be a bit of a bouncer. Adequate was probably a more accurate assessment. Rose looked tired and worn when she nearly knocked him over this morning. But after the kiss, she also looked as if she might cry.

His mother looked knowingly at him. "I have noticed the flowers you have sent her these last few days."

Oliver looked out the window, not wanting to look at his mother. He knew when he picked the red tulips this conversation would be soon in coming. "And you objected to them?"

She did not immediately answer. Oliver turned back to her, suddenly feeling like a little boy under her scrutiny.

"Did you mean what they said?"

Oliver swallowed. He knew it had been a risk to send purple violets and honeysuckle today, but it was how he felt—more so every day. She would not know their meaning, but still it made him feel better knowing he had told her his feelings.

He gave a slight nod.

"How long have you known?"

Oliver rubbed his hand across his neck. "Not long."

His mother tsked. "Why do men take so long to understand their feelings? I have seen it for nigh on a week."

The waiter set an ice in front of Hannah and then his mother.

Hannah took a large spoonful of green ice. "Mmmm." She licked her lips.

Oliver put his hand out. "Do not take such large bites, Hannah. It will bring on a headache."

His sister waved him aside, taking another unladylike bite. Her eyes widened and she dropped her spoon back into the dish. Placing her fingers at her temples, she began to rub. Once her mouth was empty, she glared at Oliver. "How did you do that? For I am sure you are behind it."

Oliver grinned and shook his head. "Perhaps this should be a lesson to you on the virtues of more ladylike behavior."

"I thought you did not wish me to be ladified, Oliver." Hannah shrugged, but he noticed her spoon held significantly less ice.

"Perhaps there is some benefit to you learning to be a lady." Oliver raised a brow at her and she giggled.

His mother's attention again turned back to him. "Do you know her feelings?"

Oliver lifted his shoulders and dropped them. "I believe she may feel something similar, but I believe I may have been mistaken."

His mother took a small bite, giving Hannah a pointed stare.

Hannah pulled her spoon from her mouth. "If you are speaking of Rose and how you love her, you need not talk in such vagueness. I am not as daft as you believe me to be." She took another bite, opening her mouth before it was empty. "I do have eyes, you know."

The dowager placed her spoon in her dish. "Eat your ice, dear. This is not your concern."

Hannah sighed, a pout pulling down her lips. But it was short lived as she spooned more ice into her mouth.

"When are you going to tell her the meaning of the flowers you give?"

Oliver shrugged. "When I am more certain of her feelings."

A look of concern crossed his mother's face. "The matrons have been speaking of her."

Oliver nodded. "I am aware what the *ton* has to say of her. Why do you think I have been declining invitations? I will not subject her to their disdain. Her current situation is not of her making." Oliver grimaced internally. His mother did not know the whole of Rose's story. At first, Oliver had wondered if he could love a woman who had done what she had to her sister. In the end, he knew she was changing. She was not the same lady who had helped that man take the duchess to Gretna. She was not even the same lady he had married nearly a month ago. But the *ton* did not know that part of the story. They were judging her based on the circumstances beyond her control.

His mother nodded. "Hannah told me of your interaction with Miss Carlyle." His mother shook her head. "The girl is a brute. It is what the matrons are saying that gives me concern."

Oliver's brows rose slightly. "Oh? You are not listening to the gossips, are you mother?"

She scowled at him. "She is my daughter-in-law, Oliver. I do not like what people are saying of her, but what if there is truth in their words?"

"What are they saying?" Oliver sat back and folded his arms across his chest.

His mother leaned forward, her voice dropping to a whisper. "Lady Chatsworth implied Rose had conspired to have the duchess killed."

Oliver's eyes widened and he sat forward, slapping the table with his hand. "It is lies," he hollered.

Several people at surrounding tables stopped talking and looked at him.

His mother raised one brow, her mouth set in a firm line.

Oliver slowly leaned back in his seat.

"I realize the gossips may not be entirely correct in their stories, but they often have at least an element of truth." The dowager's voice held a note of concern.

Oliver's jaw worked, his teeth beginning to ache with the pressure. "Rose and I do not have secrets. She has told me the whole of her story and I can assure you she did not try to have the duchess killed." He looked at his mother through narrowed eyes. "I should hope next time you hear the story, you put an end to it."

His mother nodded her head. "I already did. But I thought you need be aware of what is being bandied about."

"Thank you for telling me, but please, do not share this ridiculous story with Rose."

Only then did he notice Hannah had stopped eating. "How could they say such a thing about Rose? She is far too kind to do as they are saying." Hannah scraped the last of the ice from her dish, licking every drop from her spoon.

Oliver looked at Hannah. "You are not to repeat what you heard here, Hannah. Do you understand?"

Hannah nodded, her eyes wide. "I should never. Rose is my sister, after all."

Oliver's jaw continued to work. How had such a story come out? Unless the duke or duchess had shared it. Perhaps he should pay the duke a visit tomorrow and demand to know if he or his wife were responsible.

CHAPTER 19

"Mary, I know you did not steal my pearls."

Rose looked at the girl in the mirror. Mary did not look up or reply.

"Did you hear me, Mary? I know you did not steal my pearls."

"Yes. I heard you. Thank you, my lady." Mary continued to fix Rose's hair, still not meeting her gaze.

Why was she still acting guilty? Rose knew who had taken them, but something in the way Mary acted made her think Mary was still hiding something. Rose shook the notion off.

Rose glanced over at the pale-yellow dress Mary had chosen. Her nose flared slightly. Why had she ever picked such a horrid color? "Mary, I think I should like to wear the light green dress. It looks better with my complexion and eyes."

"But this dress brings out the gold in your hair." Mary pushed the last pin into place.

Rose raised a brow. There were still times when Mary forgot her place as maid, reverting to their childhood ways.

"Begging your pardon, my lady. Of course, I shall fetch the green one." Mary picked up the yellow dress and returned to the dressing room.

She returned a moment later with a pale green dress with tiny white flowers.

Rose scanned her room, still full of flowers. Oliver continued to send her flowers daily. Rose did not know what to make of yesterday's arrangement. The violets and honeysuckle looked pleasing together, but what had he meant with it? Were the violets a hint about her delayed visit to apologize to Violet? She guessed he'd sent the honeysuckle because he remembered her mother had loved it, but the violets she could not understand.

The flowers say it best. O

The note gave no explanation either.

Mary tied the sash at Rose's back and bent to pick up the night dress she had tossed onto the bed.

Rose moved over to the bouquet. Regardless of what it meant, it still smelled lovely. She bent and breathed in the smell of her mother and Violet combined. It brought back feelings of being loved, before she and Violet had drifted apart.

"Will you be needing anything else, my lady?"

"No, Mary."

The girl curtsied and left through the dressing room.

Rose took one last deep breath of the honeysuckle before turning and leaving her chambers. She had taken a tray instead of going to the breakfast room. She both wanted and did not want to see Oliver.

After his kiss yesterday, she did not know what to say to him. Had he only kissed her to keep her from being angry about the pearls? Or was there something more to it? She shook her head. That did not seem entirely right. Had she not already kissed his cheek and told him she was not angry with him? She could not account for why he had done such an intimate thing unless he was developing feelings for her. But she could not bring herself to believe such a thing could be true. He knew too much of her character. Still, she had not schooled her heart where he was concerned and until that happened, she was wary of spending too much time with him.

Rose retrieved her bonnet and gloves. "Hollings, is the carriage ready?"

"Yes, my lady. James will see you to Heatherton House, but then he will return and collect his lordship."

Rose scowled. "What if I should wish to come home before James has come for me?"

"He will make haste, my lady. You needn't worry."

What choice did she have? Rose bit her lip. What if Violet should throw her out? It was unlikely, but after all Rose had done, Violet would be within her rights. But Violet had not the temperament Rose did.

"Very well, Hollings. If it is the best that can be done."

Rose finished tying the ribbon of her bonnet with hard, jerky movements and waited by the front door for Francis to open it.

Once inside the carriage, Rose sat back against the seat. Her stomach twisted and lurched as she thought of what she was about to do. Would Violet even accept an apology? She thought back on their interaction just a few days past, and Rose grimaced.

Over the last few days, Rose's thoughts had bounced between Oliver and his kiss and Violet.

While she wanted to believe the kiss was genuine, her mind would not allow it.

When Rose thought about all the events leading up to Violet's kidnapping, it made her stomach roil to think on what she had done. Had the roles been reversed, Rose did not know if she could have forgiven Violet, let alone sponsor her for a

Season. It only proved what a better person Violet was than Rose.

When had she changed into such a wicked person? It really did not matter when it had happened. What was done was done and now she needed to make amends.

She sighed. The lack of sleep the past few nights was finally settling on her, making her feel exhausted.

The carriage stopped and Rose waited for the door to open, her nervousness increasing with every second.

After what seemed an eternity, the carriage door opened and James handed her out. Rose made her way to the front door and knocked. She noticed the shake in her hand and pulled it to her front, intertwining it with her other hand.

Billings opened the door and bowed slightly. "Lady Munsford."

Rose smiled. Even her lips felt as though they were shaking. She suddenly didn't know if she could go through with this, but she pressed forward. "Good morning, Billings. Is Her Grace about?"

Billings looked at Rose with suspicious eyes but continued down the corridor. "Follow me, my lady."

They walked to the lavender room where Rose had visited with Violet the last time she came. Only this time, Violet was not within. Perhaps it was to be expected when one did not send a card by first.

"Please be seated. I shall inform Her Grace you are here."

Rose nodded. When the door shut behind her, she realized, for the first time, she felt no anger upon hearing her sister's title. Perhaps she *was* changing, becoming the person she had once been. Rose relaxed a fraction.

She looked around, noticing the lack of fresh flowers in the room. What her own townhouse lacked in sophistication and elegance, it surely made up for in color and scent.

The door opened and Violet entered. Rose stood. She noticed Violet did not smile and tension pulled down Rose's neck and shoulders.

"Good morning, Rose. You look lovely today." Violet looked Rose up and down, her head tilting slightly. Her gaze held no disdain. Her comment was in earnest. "The color suits you."

Rose smiled. Perhaps she could do this. Violet had always been amiable, and Rose had no reason to believe today would be different.

"Thank you, Violet. I could say the same of you."

Violet stood behind the chair sitting across from where Rose stood. Rose looked expectantly at Violet, knowing she should not sit before Violet. But Violet remained standing.

"I assume there is a reason for your visit?" Violet's voice held a note of caution.

Rose looked again to the chair. "Would you mind terribly if we sat?" Did Violet hear the shake in Rose's voice?

Violet nodded and sat on the edge of her chair, her back rigid. Not what Rose had hoped, but more than she expected.

She took a deep breath. "I wanted to tell you I forgive you."

One brow rose on Violet's brow, her mouth opening slightly. Rose leaned forward; afraid Violet might leave before she had the chance to finish.

"Perhaps I should have started with the apology. Please, don't leave until I have finished."

Violet closed her mouth, but she did not sit any further back in her seat.

Rose hurried on before Violet changed her mind. "I have blamed you for everything which has happened to me these last months. I did not believe you in love with His Grace. I told myself you were only pretending so he would marry you instead of me—

that you were selfish and if you had cared for me, you would have let me marry him, regardless of his feelings for you."

Violet finally sat back in her chair. Her face was a mask of indifference. She had learned the role of duchess since arriving in London. How had Rose not seen how well suited her sister was for the task before? *Because I did not wish to see it.*

"Over the past several days, I have come to realize I was wrong—very wrong. I see now how much you love His Grace, but because you loved me also, you tried not to love him. That must have been very difficult for you."

Violet nodded, but her mouth remained shut.

"I was the one who was selfish, even though your ultimate decision to marry him ruined any chance I had for another Season. For that, I forgive you."

Violet's mouth opened but Rose rushed on. "I'm not done yet. I also need to beg *your* forgiveness. I understand I am asking far more than I have given, far more than I deserve. What I did with Mr. McPhail," Violet's head ticked slightly to the right at the sound of his name, "it was unforgivable, and I am ashamed to have done it." Rose swallowed hard. It was almost over and then she could return to her chambers and crawl into bed. "Somewhere along the way, I forgot what it felt like to be loved. I know Mama loved us both, but I took her love for you and warped it into something it was not. I convinced myself she showed you more love than me, because she knew that the questions about Papa being your father would cause you trouble later." Rose's voice hitched. "I never defended you when Miss Carlson called you awful names. I am sorry I did not protect you better."

Rose stared at her hands. She wanted to look at her sister, but she was afraid what she would read in her expression. They did not talk often of Violet's pedigree. Would bringing it up now be what caused her to throw Rose out of Heatherton? No sound came from her sister.

"I see now that her love for each of us was the same in intensity, it was just different. She loved you for your similarities to her, for your shared love of music. She loved me for my differences to her, for my desire to be liked and respected." Rose gave a mirthless laugh. "Only now do I understand that irony." She took a deep breath. "I am sorry, Violet. So very sorry. I understand I need to do more to prove myself to you, before you will trust me again, but I want you to know I am trying. I am trying to be the person you can respect again. I am trying to be more like you." Rose's throat tightened, eliminating the chance for her to say anything more.

Violet stared at her.

Rose scooted to the edge of her seat, ready to push herself to standing. Perhaps she could leave before Violet called for Billings.

Slowly, a smile formed on Violet's lips and she stood, coming to sit next to Rose on the settee. She picked up Rose's hands and pulled her into an embrace. "Of course, I forgive you, Rose. Nothing has been more difficult than knowing we were at odds. I have missed you."

Rose collapsed into her sister's arms. "But how? How can you forgive me and so quickly?"

Tears pooled in the bottom of Violet's lids. "I have been praying this moment would come. I promised if you should ask for forgiveness, I should do it without question." Violet's breath caught. "I want my sister back. I am so tired of being lonely." She sniffed. "Tad is very good company, but it is not the same as a sister. He knows nothing of ribbons or lace." She grinned through the tears running down her cheeks.

Rose laughed and reached for her sister again, hugging her tightly.

After a moment, Violet pulled back, a large grin on her face. "What, pray tell, brought these realizations on love to pass?"

Rose blushed and frowned.

"What is it, Rose? When last you were here, I thought you were warming to Lord Munsford."

Rose nodded. "I am—have. But I fear I have opened myself up for pain. There are times when I believe he may love me, but...."

"But what?" Violet looked as confused as Rose felt.

"I don't know. I cannot put my finger on it. I just feel there is something wrong." She rubbed her hands together. "He is the one who took my pearls."

Violet's eyes widened. "No. It can't be true. Are you sure? Perhaps the person who told you was mistaken. I cannot imagine he would do such a thing."

Rose slumped against the seat back, dropping her head back. "I saw it with my own eyes. He told me I had a letter from Papa in his office and I could fetch it. I saw the bag in his drawer." Rose rubbed at her forehead with her thumb and forefinger. "When I confronted him, he told me he had taken them so he could have the necklace repaired. As a surprise."

Violet took her hands again. "But you do not believe him?"

Rose shrugged. "I do believe him." She thought back on the hurt in his eyes when she had accused him.

Violet shook her head. "I do not understand. What is the problem?"

"What if it is all an act? But I cannot understand what he has to gain by it."

"Why should he pretend to love you, Rose? It makes no sense. He must be in earnest." Violet's brow crinkled in thought.

Rose shook her head. "Before I married, you lived with me those six months. You know how I have been. And he knows everything, Violet. He even knows about Gretna. How could someone as good as Oliver, possibly love someone like me? I cannot account for it. And it worries me."

Rose thought of the kiss they had shared just the day before. She lifted her hand, touching her lips gently. His motivations were not the only things she was worried about. She worried how she would recover once she found out the truth.

CHAPTER 20

Oliver left Heatherton House, waving the carriage to go on without him. He needed to walk and to think. He had asked the duke if either he or the duchess were responsible for the stories now circulating about Rose. The duke flatly denied it, insisting if they had wished to reveal those details, they would not have waited so long to voice the truth.

Oliver had no reason to doubt the duke's words.

His feet carried him, without much thought, to Brooks. Oliver bounded up the stairs and headed to his favorite chair, grateful to find it empty.

If the duke and duchess had not been circulating the rumors, who had? Who even knew of it, but them? No one, from what Rose had told him.

Lord Timothy sat down in the chair across from him. He stretched his long legs out in front, crossing his feet at the ankles.

"Oliver. You have been scarce here the past few days. Do not tell me you are too happily leg shackled to join us here, anymore."

Oliver smiled. "Perhaps there is an element of truth to your words, Tim."

His friend grinned. "I am happy to hear it. But the grimness of your countenance belies your words."

"I am in earnest. It is not my marriage which has me grim." He cringed slightly at the lie. He had always been honest with Lord Timothy. Why did he feel the need to lie to him now?

Oliver leaned forward, resting his elbows on his knees. He could only think on one problem for now. "I have learned of a most egregious rumor concerning my wife. I cannot account for where it started."

Lord Timothy placed his elbows on the arms of his chair, steepling his fingers. "I believe I have heard the rumor you are speaking of. I assume it is not true?"

Oliver's brow furrowed. "Of course it is not," he snapped.

Lord Timothy put his hands up in front of him. "Whoa, Munsford. I did not circulate the rumor. You need not call me out."

Oliver relaxed. "My apologies, Tim. I am just angered by the notion of it. Has Rose not suffered enough? Must she also be falsely accused?"

Tim shook his head. "No. She should not." He steepled his fingers again. "I shall ask around and see what I can discover."

Oliver sighed. "Thank you, my friend."

He sat back, allowing some of the stress to fall away from his shoulders. If anyone could discover the source of the rumor, it was Lord Timothy.

Oliver paced in front of the window of his study.

A quiet knock sounded on his door. "Come." Was it too much

to hope that Rose had come in search of him? He was disappointed when the door pushed open and Mary entered the room. Her eyes flicked about nervously.

Why could it not have been Rose invading his private space? He was still unsure where they stood. He had not seen her since he found her with the pearls. It was almost as if she were avoiding him.

Mary continued to stand by the door, looking altogether too nervous.

"Yes?" Oliver did not have an endless amount of time to wait for the girl to overcome her nerves. He had a busy afternoon. "Did you need something?"

Mary nodded, straightening her back. "I understand I am taking a great risk, but I cannot continue to lie to my mistress. She says she knows I did not take the pearls, but it is not true. I *am* the one who took them from her chambers. I cannot continue to lie to her. I will be telling her my part in your scheme when next I see her." She licked her lips and looked past Oliver at something on the wall just over his shoulder.

The more the girl talked, the more Oliver's brows rose. She was correct in assuming she was taking a great risk. For he was within his right to sack her. But he found himself more impressed with her than angry.

"If you still have the pearls, please return them to Lady Munsford. Then I should only have to confess my part in it. But if you do not, I shall be forced to reveal your part as well."

Oliver folded his arms across his chest. He believed her when she said she would not hide his role in this plan. She was loyal to her mistress, but perhaps she could be of use to him this one last time. "My wife knows I am the one who had her pearls."

Mary's face reddened. "*Had*, my lord? You have already sold them?"

Oliver folded his arms across his chest. "I told you I was to get them repaired. How dare you insinuate that I stole them like a common criminal. By coming to me, you have done nothing but endanger your place in this house. I am the master and I will not tolerate such behavior by one employed by me."

The girl's face blanched noticeably.

"While you feel it your duty to implicate me when you confess, I, on the other hand, have kept your name out of it, taking the entirety of the burden upon myself." Her gaze dropped lower and lower until it rested on her shoes. "Lest any other servant feel they can speak to me in such a manner, I must relieve you of your position and without a reference."

Mary swallowed hard, her lip quivering slightly. She raised her chin. "Very well, my lord. I understood the risk when I came. I cannot resent it now it has happened."

Oliver admired her still rigid posture. She was a proud girl, which may very well get her in trouble again if she was not careful. But it could also serve her well. For now, if sacking her did what Oliver hoped it would, he would overlook the girl's pride and rehire her once Rose made an appearance.

"You are excused."

Mary gave a short nod and turned her back to him. Her shoulders shook slightly as she hurried from the room.

Oliver's stomach twisted. He was not one to use people in such a manner, but he could see he had few other choices.

He pulled out the chair behind his desk, and sat down, his fingers drumming on the desktop as he watched the door. Moments later it swung open and his wife blew into the room like an angry wind.

Oliver stood and walked around his desk, working hard to keep the smile from his face. She was predictable and especially beautiful with the pink of anger tinting her cheeks. He wished it was not directed at him, but it was his lot today.

"How dare you sack Mary. And without a reference! Do you know how long she has been with my family?" Rose glared at him.

Oliver smiled innocently. "Ah, Rose. You have emerged from your chambers."

She narrowed her eyes at him. "I will not allow you to get rid of her."

Oliver nodded. "Very well."

"What?" Rose walked around him, glaring.

"Very well, she is not sacked." Oliver grinned. "It was the only way I could think of to draw you out of your room."

Rose stopped circling him and placed her hands on her hips. "This was all just a ruse?"

Oliver put a finger to his chin. "If you will agree to accompany Hannah and me on our outing this afternoon, she may stay."

Rose let out a long, slow breath. "Very well. Where are we to be going on this outing?" She looked at him and Oliver felt his heart beat hard in his neck and wrists. The anger was fading, as he hoped it would, curiosity taking its place.

"For a walk."

"Where?" Rose moved in closer.

"That would ruin the surprise, now, would it not?" He moved closer to her, grinning at her. "I've missed seeing you, Rose."

She shook her head, her cheeks and neck growing red. "Very well. When do we leave?"

Oliver smiled an annoyingly large smile. From the look on Rose's face, she thought it annoying also. "You have just enough time to stop Mary from actually leaving." He looked at his watch. "I expect Hannah at any moment." Oliver flicked his hand in front of him. "Hurry along, now. You know how impatient Hannah can be."

Rose cast one more glare in his direction before turning and walking toward the door with deliberately slow steps, an obvious jab at him, knowing he would have to keep Hannah entertained until she returned.

Oliver chuckled. *Touché, Lady Munsford. Touché.*

He wandered into the entryway, hoping Rose really was not intent on making him and Hannah wait overly long.

Hannah stood at the bottom of the stairs, her bonnet already tied and gloves on. He shook his head. This did not bode well for him should Rose choose to take her time.

"Oliver, there you are. Shall we go?"

"Not just yet, Hannah. Rose has consented to join us, but she is not yet ready. I told her we would wait for her."

Hannah smiled widely. "I am happy she is to join us. She has been indoors far too much of late. The sunshine shall do her good, I dare say." Hannah's foot tapped impatiently as she continued to wait.

Oliver grinned. It was a small price to pay to get Rose to join them.

Quicker than Oliver would have assumed, knowing her irritation with him, Rose appeared at the top of the stairs. As he watched her descend, he marveled at her grace and beauty, even when she smirked at him.

He extended his arm to her once she had secured her bonnet ribbons beneath her chin.

"Shall we go, then?"

Hannah nodded vigorously and Rose chuckled. "I am sorry to have kept you waiting, Hannah. It was your brother I was intent on inconveniencing." Rose tilted her head to the side, a half-smile on her lips.

Oliver raised a brow and tipped his hat to her.

Hannah looked between the two of them, her brow creased.

She shrugged her shoulders and followed them out the door and into the carriage.

They pulled to a stop outside St. Luke's Hospital. Rose turned curious eyes on him.

He shrugged and moved out of the carriage, handing both ladies out. They walked along a path that went around the hospital, following a long row of trees before the path opened up to a large pond.

Rose's eyes lit up. "This is the Peerless Pool." She looked at him and frowned. "When last I was in London, the price of admission was quite heavy. How can we afford it?"

Hannah looked at him with hopeful eyes.

"You go on and change into your swimming clothes, Hannah." Oliver shooed her toward the marble dressing vestibule and turned to Rose. "You are correct. It is quite costly."

Rose opened her mouth, but Oliver stopped her. "My father bought admission for the whole of the year, when he was still pretending we were not in financial peril." Oliver sighed, watching until Hannah entered the vestibule to change.

"I came requesting a refund, but my plea was refused." Oliver shrugged. "I figured I may as well bring Hannah, so as the money is not completely wasted."

Rose raised a shoulder slightly and turned back to look out over the embanked pool.

Hannah emerged and made her way down the marble stairs into the shallow water. She walked several rods, the water gradually coming up to her middle. She waved at Oliver and Rose.

Rose grinned widely, returning her wave.

Oliver's chest tightened. It had been days since he had earned such a response from Rose. He missed the easy way they had spoken to one another before he had ruined everything with that kiss.

"Hannah appears to be having fun." Rose's voice softened as she spoke of his sister.

Oliver was glad, even if their current relationship was complicated, at least Hannah had not suffered.

"Yes. It is times such as these I will miss when she comes of age and must start acting as a proper lady. I confess I am trying to get in as many opportunities, such as this, before that happens."

They walked quietly around the perimeter of the pool, Oliver's hands clasped behind his back and Rose's clasped in front of her. He wanted to reach for her hand, but he was now convinced she had been avoiding him. Which if she had been, surely, she would not welcome the gesture. He did not know what to say and apparently, neither did Rose, so they continued to walk in silence.

As they finished their third time around the pool, Hannah emerged from the water, going back into the vestibule to change back into her gown. They stopped by the doorway of the vestibule to wait for her.

"I wish you would have joined me. It was most refreshing." Hannah gushed as she emerged fully dressed. She grasped Rose's hands.

"Hannah, I can feel the cold of your skin through your gloves." Rose rubbed her hands over Hannah's several times. "It is not wise to allow yourself to get so cold. What if you should catch a fever?"

There was obvious concern in her voice. Oliver was both jealous and warmed by it.

Oliver led them back to the carriage. "I have a stop to make on our way home. We should be moving along."

Hannah tucked her hand into the crook of Rose's arm, wrapping her other hand around the first. "I confess, I am a bit chilled."

Oliver handed them both into the carriage, not oblivious to the fact that Hannah and Rose sat on one side of the carriage forcing him to sit opposite them. He sat back, his leg bouncing excitedly.

Rose had no idea where they were going. He hoped she would be as happy as he thought she would.

Hannah babbled about the pool as the carriage rolled along the London streets until it stopped in front of a row of shops.

Oliver stood, stooping down as he exited the carriage. He waited on the walk below, but no one emerged. He poked his head inside. "Are you not coming in?"

Rose shook her head. "I cannot see why we should. Hannah and I can wait in the carriage while you complete your business."

Oliver grit his teeth. "I should prefer you to come in with me."

Rose sighed. "What if Hannah should get more chilled? Is it truly necessary?"

It was not, but still Oliver wanted to see her face when she saw her necklace was repaired. Not that he would not be able to see her face in the carriage, but the lighting would be so much better in the shop.

"Please?" He sounded a bit like a petulant child wishing to get his way. The only thing he had neglected was stomping his foot. But if that is what it took to get Rose to come inside, so be it.

Rose huffed lightly and shook her head, muttering something about the inconvenience of getting out of the carriage.

Oliver guided her into the small jewelry shop, with Hannah trailing behind. He smiled at Mr. Stod when the little man looked up as they entered.

"Ah, my lord. Right on time."

Oliver put his hand on the small of Rose's back, gently nudging her forward. His hand heated, traveling up his arm and into his chest. She stiffened slightly, but he did not know if it was because she was affected or irritated.

They approached the counter and Mr. Stod opened a small drawer to his left. He withdrew a small velvet pouch.

Oliver smiled at Rose, but she was looking at different pieces on display about the shelves.

He took the bag from Mr. Stod and emptied its contents into his palm. The pearls shone in the candles lighting the interior.

Still Rose's attention was elsewhere.

Oliver very nearly stomped his foot at her lack of interest. He stepped behind her. "Shall we see if they still fit?" He swung the necklace over her head, settling it around her neck and fastening the clasp. He stepped to the side and tilted his head to examine it.

Rose's eyes widened as her hand came up to her neck, her fingers running gently over the pearls. Her gaze darted up to his. "My mother's pearls—they are fixed?"

Oliver nodded, strangely happy to see the tears pooling in her eyes. He watched her lips as she counted each pearl her fingers caressed. Was it normal to be jealous of pearls?

She got to the last one, bringing her hand away from her necklace. "They are all there. Were you able to purchase replacements for the ones we lost?"

Oliver shook his head. "Every one of those pearls belonged to your mother."

Her eyes widened. "But how? It would have taken hours to search the theater."

Oliver just shrugged under her penetrating stare. "The time was nothing compared to what was lost."

Rose closed her eyes, touching the gems once last time. She stepped forward, placing a hand on his cheek. His eyes wanted to close while he relished the feel of her hand touching him, but he was afraid she might bolt while he was not watching her. His hands settled on her hips.

Going up on the tips of her toes, she gently brushed a kiss to his lips. "Thank you, Oliver."

Oliver wanted to tighten his hold on her, intensify the kiss, but he remembered the last kiss they shared and loosened his hold.

Rose stepped away, her color heightened, and her eyes cast downward.

Mr. Stod gave Oliver a knowing smile.

Oliver withdrew the money from his pocket and placed it on the counter. Taking Rose by the hand, he intertwined their fingers, loving the way her hand felt inside his. "Let's go home, my dear."

CHAPTER 21

Rose leaned in and smelled the flowers sitting on her dressing table, then smiled as her eyes caught sight of the note nestled inside the blooms.

Join me for a turn about the garden? Meet me in the conservatory at three. Yours, O

Rose did not even know all the names of the flowers in her bouquet, but she did not care. It had the reddest tulips Rose had ever seen along with purple and white pansies. The deep pink frilly- petaled flowers and the lighter pink flat-petaled flowers complimented the others beautifully.

Mary worked at Rose's hair, pulling and tugging to get it into a tight knot on the back of her head. Rose looked from her flowers to her maid's reflection in the mirror. "You got the pearls out of my box, did you not?"

Mary swallowed.

"You are not in trouble, Mary. Lord Munsford is your master, now. You were only doing what he asked of you."

Mary nodded. "I'm sorry, my lady. He told me he was doing something which would make you happy."

Rose smiled into the mirror. "He did, Mary. He made me very happy." Rose opened the drawer on her jewelry box and extracted the velvet bag. She reached two fingers inside and withdrew the string of pearls. "He fixed my mother's necklace. That is why he wanted the pearls."

Mary took a deep breath. "I am happy for it."

So am I. Rose gently pulled the strand through her hand, feeling their smooth texture glide across her skin. Previously, when Rose had rubbed the pearls, it was her mother's face which had come to her mind. But now, another face invaded her thoughts, as well.

For days she had avoided him, unable to look on him knowing that she loved him but fearing he did not return her love. The necklace had changed everything. Would a man go to such trouble for someone he did not care about? Surely, he must love her. For the first time in her life, she imagined a marriage of love and it was a picture she very much wanted for real.

"I am done, my lady." Mary stepped back and allowed Rose to examine her hair.

"Beautiful as always, Mary. Thank you."

Mary nodded, a touch of a smile on her lips. "You are welcome, ma'am."

Rose glanced at the clock and gasped. "Oh, Mary. I am to be late meeting Lord Munsford if we do not hurry. Please, help me with my gown."

Mary hurried, slipping the dress over Rose's head and quickly fastening the buttons on the back.

Rose hurried from the room, not wanting Oliver to think she was not accepting his invitation.

She entered the conservatory and walked toward the door at

the rear. This room was certainly the reason Oliver had chosen to let this townhouse over the others. She supposed conservatories in London were rare, especially on Leven Street.

Oliver sat on the bench near the door, twisting the stem of a deep red rose in his fingers.

She was practically in front of him before he looked up and saw her. His face relaxed into a pleasant smile which she happily returned.

"I see you got my note." He continued to twist the rose even faster, almost as if he were nervous.

Rose nodded. "The flowers were lovely. I wish I knew what they all were."

Oliver stood and handed her the single rose he had been holding. "A rose for my Rose." He grinned a kind of lopsided grin and he shrugged. "Not the most original. I'm sorry."

Rose laughed at his sudden awkwardness. "It is such a lovely color."

"They were moss roses and cyclamen."

Rose's brow furrowed. What was he talking about?

"The other flowers in your bouquet that you did not know. They are not as common as the tulips and pansies."

Rose tilted her head to the side. How had she not realized that first night, when Lady Mayfield had forced them together, how handsome he was? Yes, his hair was always in a bit of disarray, but it only added to his charm. He was not overly thin, like so many men of her acquaintance, but neither was he soft. His shoulders were broad, and his muscular build brought a sense of safety. Rose knew no harm would come to her if he was at her side.

The more she looked on him, the more breathless she became. Shaking her head, she drew herself out of her thoughts.

Oliver looked on her with confusion before looking down at his waistcoat and pants. He ran a hand through his hair making what few parts had been laying down, now stick out in all directions.

Rose grinned and reached out a hand, running it though his hair, pushing it back into place.

He closed his eyes for a moment. He captured her hand in his when she reached the back of his head. He pulled it down and pressed a kiss to her palm, his eyes never leaving hers.

She took in a stuttering breath, unable to swallow completely. How had she doubted his feelings for her? "You said we were taking a turn about the garden?" Her voice was high pitched and quivered.

"Indeed, I did." He placed her hand in the crook of his arm. Pulling her closer to him, he placed his other hand on top of hers.

He motioned toward the door with his head. "Shall we, Rose?"

She loved hearing her name on his lips. When he had first began using her Christian name, she had thought the jumpy sensation in her stomach would subside. But it had yet to do so.

They walked out the French doors and into the overcast afternoon. Rose looked up to the sky. "Do you think it will rain?"

He nodded. "I think it likely, but hopefully it will give us a few hours before it comes."

They fell silent as he guided her around the corner of the house where the carriage was waiting. Rose looked up to Oliver in question.

"I did not specify which garden." He wiggled his eyebrows at her, his eyes dancing with excitement.

The carriage ride was short, only taking them a short distance to Harley Street. They stopped in front of a lovely town home. A small balcony hung over the first floor of the exterior, plants and flowers filling planter boxes and providing privacy from the street below.

What was this place?

Oliver nodded down the street. "If we walk down a way, we can go into the park behind."

They turned the corner and walked several rods before Oliver stopped in front of a gate. Rose was surprised he had even seen it; so covered it was in foliage. He reached through the foliage to one side and moments later the gate sprung open a crack.

Oliver grabbed the side of the gate and pulled it the rest of the way open, allowing Rose to enter first. The private park was similar to what was located behind the duke's townhouse on Grosvenor. Oliver swung the gate closed behind him and stepped up next to her. He placed his hand at the small of her back and she felt a tingle travel up her spine.

He led her to another gate just off the center of the park. Pushing the gate open, Rose walked into a garden like none she had ever seen. Her eyes could not focus on any one element, as color and texture was everywhere she looked. She glanced over at Oliver, her eyes wide.

His face held a mixture of pride and sadness.

"What is this place?" Rose asked in a whisper.

"This is Fernwood House."

"Ohhhh," was all Rose could say. This had been his family's London home for over a century. It explained the sadness she saw.

"Why did you bring me here when it obviously brings you pain?"

Oliver shook his head. "It is not painful, at least not very. I do miss it, though. But I wanted you to see this garden. To show you what I hope to create, if ever we are out from under our financial burden."

"Did you create all this?" Rose was in awe of the garden. Every plant was perfectly situated to compliment the plant or tree next to it.

Oliver shrugged. "Parts. My mother and Henry, the head

gardener, worked closely to get it to this point." He walked forward, taking her hand in his as they worked their way along the path. "The new owners of Fernwood were kind enough to grant us permission to visit the gardens." Oliver frowned. "My mother has been unable to bring herself to come. For her it *is* painful. This was her home, her sanctuary."

Rose stopped in front of a large clump of white flowers. "I love daisies. They are such a proud flower, standing so straight and tall."

Oliver bent over. Using his thumbnail and forefinger, he cut the stem of several blooms. He straightened and handed them over to Rose.

"How did you do that? Every time I try, I succeed in only bending the stem. I can never actually sever it."

Oliver gave her a slight bow. "Practice, my dear."

Rose laughed. It felt good to laugh. She realized for the first time just how unhappy she had been for so long.

They continued around the garden; at every flower they stopped to look at, Oliver would pluck a few and give them to her. Before long a large bouquet occupied her arms.

On one side of the garden, a bench sat beneath a tree of fading pink lilacs. "Are you tired? Would you care to sit down?"

Rose nodded, placing the growing bouquet of flowers on the ground next to them.

Oliver sat next to her. He gripped the edge of the bench behind him, leaning his body back slightly. He kicked his legs out in front of him and sighed.

She glanced over at him. "We can leave. I can see this is difficult for you."

He shook his head. "No. I am only sorry, Rose. I should have liked to see you oft in this garden. It is as if it was created for you."

Rose felt her cheeks heat. "Thank you. But you need not be sorry. We will get your garden. Of that, I am certain."

Oliver sat up, placing his hands on either side of himself and turning his body toward her. "You really believe so?"

Rose nodded. "You are a determined man."

Oliver chuckled. "Oh? How so, Lady Munsford?"

She angled toward him. "You saw something in me. Something you thought worth your time and effort."

Oliver raised a hand, running the back of his fingers along her jawline. "You are beautiful, Rose. I had nothing to do with that."

She swallowed, closing her eyes and enjoying the feel of his touch. But she wrenched them open, afraid it would all turn out to be a dream. "Perhaps on the outside. But inside, there was very little beauty."

He pulled her closer and leaned in. He rested his brow against hers. "The beauty was always there. I needed only to rediscover it." His voice was low and husky. He held her gaze for a moment.

Rose held her breath, hoping he would choose to kiss her again. She had ruined the last one with fear and she did not intend to do that again.

As if reading her mind, he closed the distance and covered her lips with his. They were just as soft and warm as she remembered. Rose felt him move closer, his hand moving around her waist and pulling her tighter against him.

She melted into him, having no notion of time or location. Her hand came up and her fingers threaded into his hair at the back of his neck. He took the cue and intensified the kiss.

Somewhere in the thick haze of her brain, she heard something —a growl or grunt. Was he as affected as she was?

Oliver pulled away, and Rose leaned further into him, not wanting him to stop. A whimper brought her eyes open and she realized it came from her.

She looked at Oliver. Why had he stopped? Had she done something wrong? He motioned to someplace behind her with his head. Rose turned and saw a grizzled old gardener, his brow raised, and his mouth pulled into a tight line.

Rose put her hand to her mouth and closed her eyes. Embarrassment washed over her. What must she look like to this stranger, grasping for Oliver when he pulled away from her?

Oliver grinned. "Good afternoon, Henry."

The gardener grunted and Rose realized that was the noise she had heard. The heat in her cheeks intensified. She had believed it was Oliver making that sound, thinking him so affected, he growled. She turned away from the old man, covering her face with her hands.

Oliver stood and put his hand out to Rose. "May I introduce my wife, Lady Munsford. I was showing her your grand work here."

"Seems you were showing her a bit more than me work," the man mumbled in a loud whisper.

Rose's mouth dropped open and her face heated even more. She must look as red as the roses they had passed.

Oliver chuckled. "Is that not what a man should do to his wife in a beautiful garden, Henry?"

The gardener chuckled along with Oliver. "Aye, you've got me there, my lord."

Rose did not know if she could endure any more humiliation. She stooped down and gathered up the flowers Oliver had picked for her. "If I do not get these in water soon, they shall be done for." She cringed at the sound of guilt in her voice.

Oliver smiled widely and patted the gardener on the back.

"You done good with that one, my lord." Henry said in his same loud whisper. Rose did not know if the man was nearly deaf or just thought everyone else was, but he was less then discreet.

Oliver offered his arm to Rose and raised his brows several times at Henry. "Of that notion I am fully aware. Good day, Henry."

The gardener tipped his hat at Oliver. "And to you, sir."

Oliver led her a short distance off and pulled her into a small alcove. He pulled her to a stop and turn her to face him. She could not bring herself to look at him. He must think her a wanton bit of muslin. He put a hand on each side of her face. Using his thumbs beneath her chin, he raised her head until her gaze connected with his.

"Why does it bother you that Henry saw me kissing you? We are married, Rose."

She nodded. "But it does not stand to reason I should appear to be a light skirt, unable to get enough of your kisses." She sighed and dropped her gaze again.

He rubbed his thumbs along the bottom of her jaw and her knees melted.

"You are saying, then, that you were unable to get enough of my kisses?"

She flicked her eyes up.

His eyes danced with mischief. "He cannot see us here if you should like to try again. I am sure I can oblige you."

Rose could not help herself and she laughed. "Your offer is tempting, my lord, but as I said earlier, I need to get these into water."

Oliver pulled a hand from her face and placed it over his heart. "Ah, you cut me to the core, my love."

Rose's pulse pounded in her ears. *My love?* Had he just implied he loved her?

"Very well let us get your blooms home. Perhaps when your mind is not otherwise occupied, I can continue to school you in what a man can do with his wife in a garden." He raised his brows a few times.

Rose laughed then leaned into the hand still cupping her cheek. "Hmmm. I may actually enjoy that subject."

He placed a quick kiss on the tip of her nose, and she sighed.

Leading her to the back of the garden, Oliver held the gate open, letting her out into the park. He was quiet, but every time Rose glanced over, he was grinning.

Rose did not know how her pudding legs managed to walk her back to the carriage. When she thought on the kiss, she thought she may take flight with all the fluttering she felt in her chest and stomach. Her muscles felt jumpy and tingly all at the same time. But those feelings were tempered when she thought about being caught by the gardener. Would the gardener tell the new owners of Fernwood? What would people say if they knew? She did not think her reputation could handle more scandal.

Oliver's deep chuckle sounded next to her. "You need not worry about Henry. He is nothing if not discreet. He shall not speak a word to anyone." Could he read her so well as to know what she was thinking?

Rose looked up at him, hard pressed to keep the grin from her face. "You need not be so pleased with yourself, Lord Munsford."

She tried to look sharply at him, but the expression would not come. Instead she laid her head on his arm, not even caring that her bonnet was mashed against her cheek.

"Oh, my love, I am very pleased, indeed." His words were quiet, almost drifting away on the soft breeze.

CHAPTER 22

Oliver sat at the breakfast table, his chair pushed back. He leaned to one side, a leg stretched out in front, his opposite arm resting on the table. His food was all but done, but he continued waiting for Rose to make an appearance.

He played with the tines on his fork, spinning the utensil on the table. He liked—more than liked—the change in their relationship and now he worried about losing it. Was it worth talking to her about this?

"Oliver?" Rose floated through the door, looking fresh and rested. His heart stopped for a moment and he forgot what he had wished to speak to her about.

She frowned when she studied his face. "What is the matter? You do not look well."

Oliver stood, straightening his waistcoat, trying to appear at ease. "Everything is well." He shrugged. "As well as things can be with crushing debt looming over us."

"We will work together on that. You need not shoulder the burden alone." Rose placed food on her plate, placing it on the table next to him. He waved off the footman, pulling the chair out for her and pushing it underneath her as she sat. He then retook his seat, taking in a deep breath.

"If you are well, why do you look as if you have lost your prized spaniel?" She gave him a sideways look before taking a bite of her egg.

Oliver grunted. "It is nothing, really. I was speaking with His Grace..." He paused, squinting and pulling back slightly.

Rose turned toward him with her brows raised expectantly. "Yes. And are you going to tell me of the conversation? Or are you just informing me of your acquaintance with him because if that is the case, I am not so very impressed. I am acquainted with him also."

He shrugged. "I know your tendencies where they are concerned."

Rose smiled. "I shall stay in check, Oliver. Please, continue."

He nodded, but still held himself back slightly. Her attitudes toward her sister and brother-in-law were only part of what concerned Oliver.

"The duke and duchess are attending Vauxhall this evening. It is the opening night. He thought it may be pleasant if we all went together and so he has invited us to be their guests." Again, he squinted against the expected outburst. But when none came, he continued. "I know you are not comfortable spending time among the *ton*. But before I declined his offer, I wanted to discuss it with you." Oliver shifted in his seat.

Rose chewed, a thoughtful expression on her face. "I do wish to go." She looked slightly hesitant. Was she hesitant about him or about society in general? "But if you would rather we go someplace more discreet, I am amiable to that as well."

It appeared he was not the only one uncertain of their footing in this new relationship.

Oliver shook his head. "I should love to visit Vauxhall with you. Did you visit when last you were in London? It is quite enchanting."

Rose's shoulders relaxed and she took another bite of her breakfast. Would they ever be completely comfortable with each other?

"And Violet and His Grace will be there also?" There was a hopeful tone in her voice. This was not the reaction he had come to expect.

"We will meet them there, but yes."

Rose nodded and smiled. "Then I should like to go, very much."

Oliver pushed his chair out, a deep breath coming out at the same time. He was pleasantly surprised by the way the conversation went. "We shall leave at seven. We do not want to arrive too early." Oliver stood. "The duke has invited us to dine with them in their supper box. I shall accept the offer, if you are in agreement."

Rose nodded, a spark of excitement in her eyes. "I look forward to it."

Oliver bent over, placing a kiss on her cheek. His pulse accelerated. Would there ever come a time when he did not feel excited just to be in the same room with her? Lud, he hoped not. "I am to my club, then."

OLIVER ENTERED the dim interior of Brooks's. Had it only been a month since he had come in search of refuge on his wedding day?

He entered the parlor and was delighted to see his favorite chair was empty. His day just kept getting better and better. And in a few hours, he would be at Vauxhall with his lovely wife on his arm. Oliver breathed deeply and smiled. Yes, his life had changed greatly since that day a month ago.

Lord Kent and Mr. Penderton sat down in the chairs across from Oliver. His day was not to be perfect after all. Oliver looked around. Where was Lord Timothy when he needed him.

"Munsford, I was beginning to think you had scooted off to the country so as not to have to pay your wagers." Mr. Penderton leaned back in his seat, a smug look on his face.

"I should not think of leaving before I collect my winnings, gentlemen." Oliver smirked at them.

Lord Kent threw his head back and laughed. "You think us daft? I have seen you escorting your wife about London. From what I have seen, you are not to be the one collecting winnings." He waved a hand in the air, summoning Lord Smyth and Mr. Fairchild to join them.

Oliver scooted back in his seat, running his hands down his pant legs. He looked around, trying to find someone to help even out the sides. He spotted Lord Timothy and Mr. Parkins as they entered the parlor together. The two gentlemen would do well. Oliver waved them over.

Lord Timothy shouldered his way through the men and sat in the chair next to Oliver. "Well, what do we have here?"

Oliver grunted. "These gentlemen seem convinced they are to win the wager come June."

Lord Timothy nodded. "I see."

Lord Smyth chuckled. "It never was much of a wager. We all knew who the winners would be. In point of fact, I will feel a bit guilty for taking your money." He laughed again. "But not so guilty as to give it back to you."

Oliver shrugged. What did he care what they said? He knew where he stood with Rose and he was quite happy with it.

Mr. Fairchild leaned in. "I've heard tale the chit is casting her eyes in other directions."

Oliver shot to his feet. "That is a lie and I suggest you reconsider it at once."

Lord Kent moved between the two. "Perhaps. But can you be sure?"

Oliver grunted in irritation. "I've never been more sure of anything in my life."

"Perhaps five hundred pounds apiece would show your faith in your wife." Mr. Fairchild folded his hands over his chest.

Lord Timothy stood up next to Oliver and placed a hand on his arm. "They are baiting you, Oliver. Just walk away."

Oliver jerked his arm away. He knew his wife and he had no doubt she was faithful to him. If raising the bet is what would shut down the gossip mills, so be it. Oliver would be winning the wagers, anyhow. "One does not walk away from a sure thing. Five hundred pounds apiece."

Oliver felt Lord Timothy suck in his breath beside him. Mr. Parkins muttered under his breath. They could be worried all they wanted, but Oliver knew better.

He moved with Lord Smyth and Mr. Penderton to the betting book so each could amend their wager.

THE SUN HUNG low in the sky as Oliver and Rose walked past the Temple of Cormus. It had taken longer than Oliver had anticipated to get to Vauxhall, due to the sheer number of carriages crowding the Vauxhall bridge. From the looks of the crowds, the gardens would easily attract tens of thousands of guests this evening.

Rose clutched tightly to his arm as they maneuvered through a large crowd of people watching a tight rope walker and several other dancers. "Are those the same ones we watched at Astley's?" Rose leaned her head close.

Oliver nodded his head. "I believe it likely. Although, it is possible they have several different casts."

Oliver opened his pocket watch. "If we are to make it to His Grace's box, we should increase our pace. I had no idea we would encounter such crowds tonight." Oliver sighed at his daftness. "Although, I should have considered it with it being opening night."

Rose patted his arm. "We are here to enjoy ourselves. There is no need to hurry unnecessarily. I am certain there will still be food, even if we arrive late."

Oliver smiled at her and nodded, but he did not slow his pace. He was on good terms with the duke and did not wish to earn his displeasure by forcing him to wait for them.

"Ah, here we are, number nine." Oliver looked into the empty box.

Rose looked up at him and shrugged. "See? We hurried for no reason. They are not yet arrived." What were they to do? It was not as if they could make themselves comfortable in the duke's supper box.

"Ah, Munsford. Sorry to have made you wait." The duke's voiced carried on the breeze from behind them. "The bridge was a mess of carriages. I believe I could have walked faster than that dratted carriage." He shook his head, his face set in an irritated frown.

The duke and duchess pulled even with Oliver and Rose. Her Grace shrugged, but a smile turned her lips upward. She leaned over and lightly hugged Rose.

Oliver watched, curious as to what Rose's response would be. He was surprised when she returned the duchess's embrace.

When they separated, Rose curtsied to the duke. "Thank you for inviting us to join you, Your Graces."

If anything, Rose's comment seemed only to irritate the duke more. "I will allow the formality, *Lady Munsford*," he emphasized her name, "but only because we are in public. Do not think I will stand for it when we are at Heatherton House."

The duchess grinned even wider and looked to Oliver. "Please excuse my husband. He had a most vexing day in Lords, and I am afraid the lineup of carriages on the bridge only served to heighten his irritation." She motioned to the box. "Let us eat and perhaps once he has had his fill, he will relax a little." She gave her husband a pointed look.

The duke shrugged, giving her a bland look in return. She raised a brow and his mouth began to twitch.

They moved into the box and a waiter stood ready to serve them before the men had even taken their seats. The duke ordered ham, chicken, cheeses, puddings, custards, and tarts, among other things. The waiter scurried away, and they settled back to listen as the orchestra played several Handel pieces.

"I must apologize for my earlier terseness. I have discovered I loathe London and am quite anxious for Parliament to adjourn for the summer." He looked around. "While these gardens are lovely, they are nothing to Morley Park."

The group fell silent as they continued to listen to the music filling the grounds.

The food was good, but Oliver knew they would have had better fare had they stayed at home and eaten what Mrs. Poole cooked for them. Oliver knew eating at Vauxhall was not about the food, but the surroundings.

A whistle blew and within minutes thousands of lamps glowed in the dusky light. A sigh sounded beside Oliver and he looked over to see Rose's eyes widen. "Oh, it is lovely."

"We have a few hours before the fireworks. Perhaps once we are finished eating, we could take a turn around the gardens." He leaned in close to Rose. "I understand there are several paths with much less lighting than here." He raised a brow. His pulse quickened when she colored up. The thought of being alone with her in a darkened alcove made him anxious for the food service to end.

The duke leaned back. "I should enjoy a walk also." Oliver did not miss the loving look he cast at the duchess. Oliver wondered how Rose could have believed there was no true partiality on her sister's part, for the duchess looked equally enamored of her husband. Perhaps one saw what they wished to see.

He glanced at Rose. What did she see when she looked on him? Did she still only see a fortune hunter in need of her money?

"I hope you don't mind if we separate for a time. We can meet for the fireworks and watch them together?" Violet gave Rose a knowing smile.

Oliver was still watching Rose when she turned and caught him. She smiled and answered for them both. "We should enjoy that very much."

The duke pushed out from the table and Oliver took it as his cue to do the same. He helped Rose from her seat and led her from the box and onto the Grand Walk. They passed the golden statue of Aurora, before turning off onto a smaller, more remote pathway. Here the lamps were fewer, casting the path in a dim glow, allowing for long stretches of near darkness.

"Thank you for bringing me here. I had no idea it was so magnificent."

Oliver squeezed the hand that clutched his arm. "It is no more lovely than you are, my dear."

They walked several rods in silence. "Are you going to continue to give me flowers every day for the rest of my life?"

Oliver pulled her into a darkened alcove off the path. He

leaned down, placing a kiss on her ear lobe. "Unless you tell me otherwise," he whispered in her ear. The gooseflesh that erupted on her arms was discernible even through his gloves.

He chuckled and kissed her again, this time on the neck. Her skin was soft and warming more with every kiss. He felt her swallow.

"We should not be doing this here. What if someone should see us?" Several of her words were indiscernible through her trembling breaths, but Oliver noticed she did not pull away.

"They would see a man kissing his wife. What is so untoward about that?"

"But—"

Oliver cut her off with his lips, pulling her in close to him. He wanted to tell her with words how he felt about her. He had told her with flowers and even alluded to it when he called her my love. But he had yet to form the words. He pulled back. "Rose, there is something I need to tell you."

She took another stuttering breath. "What?"

"Lord Munsford, is that you?"

Oliver felt Rose stiffen in his arms before taking several steps away.

Oliver squinted into the low-lit pathway. How had Miss Carlyle seen them, unless she had followed them from the main path? Oliver reached for Rose, but she gave a tiny shake of her head.

"And who is it you are wooing tonight?" Miss Carlyle peered into the darkness. "Miss?" Her eyes widened slightly. "Lady Munsford?" She gave a little chuckle, turning her gaze back on Oliver. "I see, my lord, you are committed to winning the wager you placed at Brooks's. Leaving nothing to chance."

Rose looked at Oliver, hurt and confusion battling for prominence. "Wager? What is she speaking of?"

"Rose-"

Miss Carlyle cut him off. "Have you not heard? Lord Munsford placed a rather large bet on the success of your marriage. I heard tale he even increased the amount, just this morning." Even in the darkened pathway Oliver could see her smirk. "It seems he will do about anything to win. But then, his family's livelihood is at stake. People take drastic measures when their way of life is in jeopardy."

Oliver turned toward Rose. He reached for her hand, but she jerked it out of his grasp. Pushing past him, she stumbled onto the path.

"Rose, wait." Oliver reached for her, grabbing her at the wrist. She shrugged away and ran back in the direction they had come.

"What the devil are you doing?" Oliver had never been tempted to land a facer on a lady, but there was a first for everything.

"I was simply putting Miss Allen in her place. She, who thought herself above us all when she was engaged to a duke." Miss Carlyle folded her arms across her chest. "Well, now she is not so lofty, is she?"

"It is *Lady* Munsford to you, *Miss* Carlyle." Oliver shook his head, his hands fisting at his side. "You have no idea what you have done. I shall see you pay for this."

Miss Carlyle shrugged. "Your position is drastically reduced, as well, my lord. Do not threaten me."

Oliver side stepped her. "Not to worry, Miss Carlyle. It is not a threat."

He turned away from her and ran down the path after his wife. His decision to increase his bet seemed less prudent with every step he took. How must this look to her? Did she really believe Miss Carlyle's inferences? Surely, Rose knew the lady was a shrew.

Oliver burst out onto the Grand Walk, nearly bumping into several people. They glared at him and he pulled up short, frantically searching the crowd.

Oh, why had he not taken her someplace with fewer people? He would never be able to find her in this crowd

CHAPTER 23

Rose picked up her skirts and practically ran down the pathway. Her cheeks burned with humiliation. How had she been such a dolt? How had she believed—she could not even finish the thought.

She pushed her way through the crowds, until she got to the supper box they had occupied earlier. It was empty. Where was Violet? She needed to find her sister.

Rose squinted through the crowd, but there were so many people. She closed her eyes. *Think, Rose.* Where would Violet go?

Besides trying to find a dark, out of the way place as Oliver had done—her chest tightened—where else would they be? The notes of the orchestra floated to her ears and Rose knew where she needed to look for her sister. Violet loved music. It was not a certainty, but it was likely. If Violet was not there, she would worry about that when it happened.

Rose moved toward the two-story rotunda where the orchestra was playing. Several benches were scattered about the grassy area surrounding it. On the opposite side, Rose spotted her sister and the duke. Shearsby sat with his legs stretched out in front of him, his ankles crossed and his arm around Violet's shoulders. Her head rested against his chest and her eyes were closed as they both listened to the music.

Rose rushed over. "Oh, Violet. There you are. I—" she paused, pushing the tears back. She could not allow them to see her cry. Or at least not the whole of the *ton* that seemed to be attending Vauxhall tonight. "I am feeling ill. Could you please take me to Heatherton?"

Violet pushed away from her husband, standing in front of Rose. She reached for Rose's hands, her brow furrowed. "Rose, what is it? You look truly ill."

Shearsby stood up next to his wife, his eyes scanning the crowd. "Where is Munsford? Did you become separated?"

Rose shook her head. "No. Please, can we just go? I will explain once we are in the carriage."

Violet glanced at her husband and he nodded. She wrapped an arm around Rose's waist, and they moved toward the main entrance.

The street outside the gates was crowded with carriages, guests still arriving for the fireworks display.

The duke found a street urchin milling about the crowd. He placed a hand on the boy's shoulder. The boy turned around, looking up at the duke's imposing form.

His Grace pulled a few coins from his waistcoat pocket and put them in the boy's hand. He showed him the signet ring on his little finger. "I am in need of our carriage. It should be located on Kensington Street. Find the carriage with this crest on the door and tell the driver to pick us up at Cumberland Gardens. Return with the driver and I will give you two more." He held up the coins.

The boy nodded his head and set off at a run. People

continued to stream in and out of the gates. Rose clung tighter to her sister. "Is there not someplace we can wait, away from prying eyes?"

Shearsby nodded. They walked a short way and entered a small garden area. "We should be away from the majority of the crowds here." He looked back at Rose. "Are you sure you do not want me to have Munsford fetched? I could send someone in after him."

Rose shook her head. "My disappearance will be of no consequence to him, I can assure you of that." Her voice hitched and she clenched her fists, digging her nails into the palms of her hand.

Rose and Violet sat on the bench; the duke chose to pace the walkway in front of them, his hands clasped tightly behind his back as he muttered under his breath.

Violet remained quiet, waiting on Rose to start the conversation.

Rose's thoughts flitted in every direction. How could Oliver do this to her? Was any of it real or was Miss Carlyle right? Had he not shown disdain for his own father's poor financial decisions? A wager was far more scandalous than the imprudent investment Oliver's father had made. Why would he do such a thing? She thought she knew him.

Rose sniffed, angrier with herself than with Oliver. Why had she let him do this to her? She had let down her guard. And all because of a bunch of flowers—a small show of kindness. Was she so desperate for love she had dismissed any signs there may have been?

After what seemed an eternity, the Shearsby carriage finally rolled to a stop. The duke waved them over from where they were sitting.

The boy hopped down from the driver's box, a wide grin on his face.

Violet helped Rose to her feet and they moved in behind Shearsby. He handed the boy the promised coins. "You seem an honest boy. If you come to Grosvenor Street on the morrow, I will see you have a job waiting for you."

The boy's eyes widened, and he nodded. "Yes, my lord."

The duke smiled and patted him on the head. "It is getting late. Go home to your mother."

It was these types of actions that had drawn Violet to the duke in the first place. He had a kind heart, even if he was gruff at times.

Rose nearly choked on a cry. She had hoped she had found such a man in Lord Munsford. Why did it have to hurt so badly to discover she had not?

"Ain't got no ma, my lord."

The duke's brow furrowed. "Then up into the driver's box with you. You can begin your service tonight."

The boy grinned and climbed back up with the driver.

The footman stood ready with the door open. Shearsby handed Rose in first, and then his wife, kissing her hand before he released it. She smiled at him. There was that look. It was a look Rose had not understood until Lord Munsford placed the pearls about her neck. He had looked on her in much the same way. Or she thought he had. But now she did not know.

Something told her there was no acting going on between the duke and her sister. Was it possible Oliver was not acting either? What was it Miss Carlyle had said? *I see Lord Munsford, you are committed to winning the wager you placed at Brooks's.* She had said he was leaving nothing to chance.

Rose looked away from them before the interaction undid her.

Violet took her seat next to Rose. "You do not need to cut your evening short, Violet. You and Shearsby may stay and watch the fireworks." She leaned her head against the window. "I can manage on my own."

"Nonsense. Tad purchased an annual pass for the gardens. We can see the fireworks another night."

The carriage leaned to one side as the duke's large frame climbed in. He settled himself and knocked on the side. The carriage began its slow progress home. To Violet's home, anyhow.

Once they were underway, Violet turned to Rose. "Now, tell me what is wrong. I thought you and Lord Munsford were getting on quite well."

"I am a fool. I believed a show of kindness and a few stems of flowers equated to love." Not allowing the tears to fall seemed to direct all the moisture to her nose. It began to run, and she wiped at it with the back of her hand.

Violet handed her a handkerchief. "You are not a fool. Most ladies would think such a thing." Rose saw Violet glance at her husband. "Are you sure his feelings are impartial? I saw the way he looked at you over supper, Rose."

Rose laughed mirthlessly. "Yes, I saw it too. Or I thought I did. But it was all an act, for the sake of a bet."

"Damnation." The duke slapped his hand on the bench next to him. "I had heard rumors. But I disregarded them. I thought I knew the man's character." He looked at Violet with large eyes. "I had him thoroughly investigated. He was not a gambler, at least not that Dawson could discover."

"Why does this wager mean he does not care for you?" Violet looked utterly confused.

The duke cleared his throat. "The bet was based on the success of his marriage. If the two of them proved to get on well, he would win. If not, he would pay."

Violet frowned. "But how does one prove such a thing as love?"

"By the looks one gives his wife, I suppose." The duke's voice dropped, and he looked at his hands.

The sob Rose had been holding in since hearing Miss Carlyle's accusations forced its way out.

Violet pulled her close to her side, her hand rubbing circles on Rose's back. "I'm sorry, Rose. I had thought you had finally found happiness."

Rose wiped at her nose with Violet's linen. "I thought I had also. But I was wrong."

She laid her head on her sister's shoulder. At least one good thing had come out of this disastrous marriage. She had Violet back.

CHAPTER 24

The sun streamed through the windows, shining directly into Rose's eyes. She put her arm over her face, blocking out the blinding light. She peeked out from under her arm, realizing she was in her room at Heatherton House. Each morning for a week, the same realization hit her and along with that realization came memories of that night.

Rose had wished several people to Hades in her life—Violet among them, not long ago—but no one as much as she wished Miss Carlyle now. The woman had destroyed what had otherwise been a perfectly lovely evening and possibly even her marriage.

And as much as her head wanted to wish the same fate she wished for Miss Carlyle on Lord Munsford, her heart would not allow it.

Rose touched her lips. They burned with the awareness that his kisses had not been sincere. She wiped her hand back and forth across them, trying to wipe the kisses away. But it was for naught. When she closed her eyes, she could still feel his lips on hers.

Rose threw back the covers, even though she knew not the

point of getting up. What had she to do today that required her to leave her bed?

Mary came into the room with a tray. The smell of hot chocolate drifted to Rose's nose. Chocolate was what the duke had every morning. He said he could not stand the weakness of the English tea. He had brought the chocolate back from the West Indies with him. Rose did not care for it plain, but if she added a little cream and a spoon of sugar, it was quite good.

"Good morning, Mary."

"Good afternoon, *Rose*." Mary's mouth set in an unhappy line at the use of Rose's Christian name. She did not know why Mary was so decidedly against using it. After all, Mary had called her Rose every day of her life before becoming her lady's maid. But Mary would have to get used to it. Rose could not hear Lady Munsford yet, not without her chest tightening.

Mary studied Rose as she placed the tray on the bedside table. "You do not look well. Perhaps you should stay abed today."

Rose swallowed and shook her head. "Nothing good is coming from me lying about. I believe some time in the garden will serve me better. I need some air. Please, help me dress."

"Very good. If that is what you wish."

Rose gave one firm shake of her head. "It is what I wish."

Mary took a bouquet of red chrysanthemums, pink carnations and orange honeysuckle and placed it on the window ledge. The bouquet had clumps of clover tucked between the flowers, making the colors appear even more vibrant. Her room was scattered with flowers, a new bouquet having arrived every morning and sometimes a second one in the afternoon. Only the one sent on the first day after Vauxhall had held a note. *Please, let me explain. O*

Rose had crumpled it up and thrown it in the rubbish bin. But then in a moment of weakness, she had retrieved it and smoothed it out as best she could. The note was now tied with all the others he had sent her over the last month. She kept them all neatly tucked away in the drawer of her jewelry box that Mary had brought with her. In the late-night hours, when it was most quiet, she would devour those letters. Looking for hints that she should have expected this.

She had never replied to the note, though. And no new notes had come. Just the flowers.

Rose moved over to the tray, needing the chocolate to help cure her of the sluggishness she felt. A package wrapped in brown paper took up most of the tray.

Mary came in with Rose's gown, draping it over the end of the bed.

"Mary, what is this?"

Mary glanced at the package. "A footman asked me to deliver it to you. It came sometime this morning, but there was no card on the outside. Perhaps it is wrapped up with whatever is inside."

Rose slipped the twine from around the package and pulled the paper off. A book of drawing paper and a set of charcoal pencils sat in her hand. A small card sat atop the charcoals. *Perhaps now you will have time to try your hand at sketching. Yours, O*

Rose did not know whether to throw them in the rubbish bin or hug them to her chest. Did this not prove he truly cared for her? Her heart screamed it did. But her mind continued to object. Would he not do anything to win those wagers?

She put the charcoals to the side and sat down at her dressing table. Mary set to work, readying her to face the day.

Rose shut the door of her chambers behind her, walking quietly down the corridor. Mary had done her best to make Rose look presentable, but still her skin looked pale and there were dark circles visible under her eyes.

Rose pushed out onto the large stone terrace, the large tree to the side shielding much of the area from the sun. She looked out over the gardens. Heatherton House's garden was beautiful, but it did not have the same charm as the gardens at Fernwood.

Rose stepped down onto the pebbled path, clutching the paper and charcoals to her side. Most of the tulips were long since cut down, making way for the summer blooming flowers. But one lone pink tulip stood, as if reminding her what she had lost.

Rose found the bench in the garden and sat on the grass, leaning her back against it. She flipped to the first page of the book. The blank page stared up at her. What was she to do with it? What should she sketch?

She looked out over the gardens, sketching lines and curves on the paper. She paused and looked down at what she had drawn. The old Rose would have found numerous faults with this piece of art, but new Rose could see the simple beauty in the monochromatic picture. When she looked at it, she could see the colors in her mind. What would she be able to create had she oils at her disposal?

Rose plucked a purple geranium, fingering the soft petals. When she came to London, she'd had no notion of the names of most flowers—tulips, roses and honeysuckle being the only ones to claim that prize. Now, just over a month later, as she looked over the garden, she could name more than a dozen different flowers such as the iris, hollyhocks and ivy. Had it only been such a short time since her marriage? Less than two months to fail miserably as a wife.

A leaf crunched on the path and Rose turned to find Violet and the dowager standing a way off. Rose put her drawing on the bench and pushed herself to standing.

Violet smiled stiffly. "Rose, you have a guest." Her eyes widened slightly, and her mouth clenched shut. A small smile appeared on Rose's face at her sister's silent apology. "She was quite adamant about seeing you."

Rose nodded. "Lady Munsford. I was not expecting you." She had hoped Oliver would come. In her dreams he came to beg her forgiveness and swear his undying love. But her dreams never came true.

"You also have another delivery of flowers in the house. I'll have them sent to your chambers." Violet clasped her hands together and leaned in close. "If you wish me to stay, I will."

Rose's stomach flopped. She wanted very much for Violet to stay, but Rose knew she needed to handle this herself. She needed practice standing on her own. It was probable she would be sent to the country estate to live alone.

"We will be well, Violet. You can return to the house. Lady Munsford and I have no qualms with each other." Rose did not feel the truth of her statement. At the moment, she felt very much at odds with her mother-in-law.

Violet sighed, raising a brow as she cast one last look at the dowager. "Very good. Thomas will be waiting on the terrace should you need anything." She reached out and gave Rose's hand a quick squeeze before she dropped it and returned to the house.

"I know it is very improper of me to call without sending around a note first." The dowager twisted the corner of the linen she held in her hands. Rose quirked her head to the side. Was she just as nervous about this conversation as Rose was?

"I was afraid you would decline should I ask in advance." The lady looked out over the garden and her body relaxed.

Rose understood that feeling.

"Her Grace has a very lovely garden, here."

Rose nodded. "Yes, although I do not believe it was as well thought out as Fernwood."

Lady Munsford smiled. "Oliver told me the two of you visited Fernwood. I am happy it was to your liking."

"Very much so." Rose stooped down to the bench to pick up her sketch. Lady Munsford reached out a hand, grasping the opposite side of the book. "Did you sketch this? I was not aware you enjoyed drawing."

Rose shrugged. "Nor was I. I only just received these today. I have not done much sketching before now."

Lady Munsford turned and looked out over the garden and then back at the drawing. "You are very good, my dear. I should never have guessed you had not been practicing for years."

Rose blushed and ducked her head. "Thank you, my lady."

The dowager sighed. "Did we not decide upon Mama?"

Rose rubbed at the charcoal on the paper with her thumb. Was using the intimate name a prudent idea, under the circumstances?

The two started walking, neither speaking for a time.

Lady Munsford stopped in front of a cluster of carnations. "I love flowers. I inherited that trait from my father. He is the one who taught me about plants."

"Yes, Lord Munsford told me." Rose nodded. "I did not realize how much I liked them until recently." She glanced over at her mother-in-law. "It surprised me that something so simple could change my mood so quickly."

Lady Munsford opened her mouth and then closed it. Was she unsure of what to say or did she know what she wished to say, but did not know how Rose would accept it? The lady gave an almost imperceptible nod of her head. "Did you know flowers have a language all their own?"

Rose's brow wrinkled. "I do not understand. You are not implying that flowers can speak, are you?" Was the lady not right in the head? Rose had never seen any signs of madness before, but Lord Munsford had mentioned his mother often talked to plants.

Lady Munsford chuckled. "No." She glanced over at Rose. "You need not plan for my removal to St. Luke's just yet."

Rose heard the humor in her voice as the lady grinned down at the flowers.

"What I mean to say is each flower symbolizes something—an emotion or thought. The language of flowers has been in existence for centuries. Shakespeare speaks of it in Hamlet. For example," she pointed down at the carnations, "if I were to give you the pink one, I would be telling you that I will never forget you. While the red ones would tell you that my heart aches for you."

What was she talking about? Did she believe that flowers sent specific messages?

They began walking again, taking a slow pace as they both looked at the flowers. "The geranium you have in your hand symbolizes friendship. And those daisies mean hope." She took a deep breath. "It is not just flowers, either. Clover, ivy and holly, all mean something when in a bouquet."

Rose stopped walking. Could all the bouquets Oliver had given to her have meant something specific? Something more than just pretty colors and lovely smells? Rose thought back on the flowers she had received this morning. "You said that pink carnations symbolize something different than red. Is that always the case?"

Her mother-in-law nodded. "In most cases. Red, in every flower I can think of, symbolizes passion and deep love, while white usually symbolizes purity and innocence or sweetness. Although, it can also symbolize a new beginning." They moved past a trellis full of honeysuckle blossoms. "Sometimes the receiver must interpret which definition is correct, based on the most recent events in their life."

Rose looked at the deep orange blossoms. "What of the honey-suckle? What does the sender say with it?" Lord Munsford had sent her honeysuckle on several occasions. She had always assumed it was because he knew her mother loved the flower. But was that the only reason?

"Ah, the honeysuckle. One of my favorites." Lady Munsford leaned forward, taking in a deep breath.

Rose picked a flower from the vine and pulled the stamen from the center, sucking out the nectar from it. "It was my mother's favorite, also. My father bought her perfume that smelled of the flower so she could smell it even in the wintertime."

The dowager looked wistful. "The honeysuckle symbolizes bonds of love, so while your father may not have realized it, his gift was telling your mother that their love could never be broken."

Rose crossed her arms across her middle. Had her father realized that was what his offering meant? While she did not believe he knew what honeysuckle symbolized, she did know he loved her mother and their love had not ended with her death. It was something she had never thought on before, but now that she considered it, it made her breath stop.

What of her husband? Did he feel their love could never be broken? Did he even believe they had love?

Lady Munsford placed a hand on Rose's arm. "Do you understand what I am telling you? I know you believe Oliver has used you very ill, but I have seen the flowers he has given you. He did not choose them only because he thought them pretty. They were selected deliberately—with great thought."

Even though her arms were folded, Rose could feel her hands shaking. Could Lady Munsford be telling the truth? Did Oliver mean what his mother was saying the flowers symbolized? Rose tightened her arms, hugging herself more completely. She didn't know if she dared open herself up again. Especially if there was a chance it would end in disappointment. Her heart thumped quickly.

"Please, Rose, come home. Hannah and I miss you greatly." The dowager bit her lip. "But not nearly so much as Oliver does."

"If he misses me so, why has he not come to see me?"

A confused look came across her mother-in-law's face. "He has come every day. Who do you think brings the flowers you receive? Each time he is turned away."

"By whom?"

"The butler, I assume."

Rose smiled sadly. It appeared Shearsby was trying to make amends, in his own way, for forcing her into this marriage. The irony was he need not make amends. Even with the way things were now, she did not believe she would change anything if the opportunity were there.

"I am not agreeing to come back, nor am I disagreeing. I need to think on what you have said." Part of her wanted to leave this moment and go see Oliver. But even if she looked into his eyes and saw love, could she trust it?

Lady Munsford nodded. "I understand. Thank you for seeing me."

Rose stayed in the garden for a long time. She had never heard of flowers meaning specific things, but she had not paid flowers much heed before. As she reviewed all the bouquets she had received, a new picture began to form in her mind. If what the dowager said was true, Oliver had been telling her for weeks that he loved her.

One question still lingered. How much money had he wagered? Was that the only reason why he was acting the part of a besotted husband?

She walked back to the house and knocked on the duke's study door.

"Enter."

Rose pushed the door open and tentatively stepped inside. This room had not seen many civil conversations between Rose and Shearsby.

"Can I do something for you, Rose?"

Rose nodded. "Do you know how much my husband wagered on our marriage?"

The duke sat back in his seat, his elbows resting on the arms of his chair, his fingers steepled in front of his chin. "Between the two wagers? One thousand pounds."

Rose sucked in a breath. "That is a great deal of money." She sat in the chair opposite the duke. "You said there were two wagers?"

The duke nodded. "Yes. Five hundred pounds apiece." He bounced his steepled fingers on his chin. "The original wagers were four hundred a piece. Then last week, on the morning we went to Vauxhall, the wagers were increased to five."

Rose was not sure what to think. He was either very confident or very daft. It was the day after they had visited Fernwood's gardens. Rose thought back on their kiss. Confidence was certainly what he was feeling. He should have had no doubt as to her feeling for him. Why should he not have increased the bet when it was so certain he would have won?

"If you want my opinion—" Shearsby paused, as if waiting for her to object. When she did not, he continued. "I believe he increased the wager because he knew he would win. And not because he had tricked you. I think he knew how he felt and believed you likely felt the same." He sat forward in his seat, moving his elbows to his desk. "It is the first and last bet he has made. And he wagered it all on you."

Rose swallowed hard. *Oh lud. I have made a terrible mistake.* She moved to stand but dropped back down into the chair. "I understand Lord Munsford has visited every day. Do you know on whose orders he has been turned away?"

Shearsby breathed deeply. "It was on my orders. Until I knew for certain his character, I did not want him in my home."

Rose bit her lip. "Did you consider my feelings in your decision?"

The duke nodded a small grin on his lips. "The man needed to suffer for a time, but he has suffered enough. If you feel inclined to see him, I shall not object."

Rose gave a slight grin and stood up. "Thank you for your opinion. I shall take it under advisement."

She twisted at her fingers until they lacked any blood in them. "I have apologized to Violet. But I must also do so to you." She took a calming breath and raised her chin. If she was to do this, she would do it properly. "I behaved most badly. I am ashamed to even think upon it. I know my words will never be enough, but I hope they are a start and I can begin to earn back your trust."

"Yes, Violet told me of your visit. She is grateful to have back your friendship. It has been difficult for her."

Rose nodded. "I have missed her, also." She bit the inside of her cheek. Did this mean he was unable to forgive her?

"You are correct, it will take time to heal, but I forgive you, Rose."

She smiled. "Thank you, Your Grace."

He grinned back at her. "You may call me, Tad. I find I do not mind the informality."

Rose nodded. She turned and walked from the room, even though every impulse told her to run. She went quickly to her chambers and pulled out a paper and quill.

Mama,

Please meet me at the flower cart on St. James Street at 9 on the morrow. Do not speak of this to Lord Munsford or Hannah. Send word if this does not meet with your approval.

Yours,

Rose

She pulled the bell for Mary and waited, her foot tapping impatiently on the imported Persian rug. Finally, the door opened, and Rose thrust the note into Mary's hand. "Please see this is delivered to the Dowager Lady Munsford immediately. It is of utmost importance."

Mary nodded and turned toward the door.

"Hurry, Mary. There is no time to lose." Rose snapped.

The maid scurried from the room while Rose sat and waited for morning to arrive.

CHAPTER 25

Oliver waited on the porch of Heatherton House for the butler to open the door. Every day for a week he had come with a bouquet of flowers, hoping this was the day Rose would see him.

The butler opened the door. Was that pity in his eyes? Oliver was beyond caring. Every day she was gone from his life, his heart ached a little more. He had known he loved her that night at Vauxhall, but he had not realized just how much until she had fled.

"I am sorry, my lord, but Lady Munsford is not home to visitors."

You are correct. She is not at home—not at our home, anyhow, Oliver mumbled as he thrust the bouquet forward. The entire arrangement was red. Red geraniums, red roses, red carnations. It was the only way he could tell her how much he loved her, without seeing her.

"Is that Munsford at the door, Billings?"

The door opened wider and the duke reached his hand out to Oliver. "Come in, Munsford."

Oliver allowed himself to be pulled into the entryway. His pulse quickened at the thought of catching a glimpse of his wife. His eyes scanned the staircase and upper landings.

The duke chuckled. "She is not here, Munsford. You will not be catching a glimpse of her *here*." He raised a brow. "Unless you were looking for someone else."

Oliver's shoulders dropped. Then why even be in here, if not to see Rose? "I should be on my way. I only came to bring her flowers."

The duke folded his arms across his chest. "How long do you have left on the wager?"

Oliver ran a hand over his face. Gah. That blasted wager! Why had he ever thought it a good idea? "The end of the Season." At this point in time, Oliver did not think the rest of his life would be enough time to get Rose to speak to him, let alone fall in love with him.

The duke nodded. "Ah, very good."

Very good? How could anything about this be very good? Oliver narrowed his eyes. "I do not know what you are about, Your Grace—"

The duke held up his hand. "Shearsby, remember? We are brothers now."

Oliver shook his head in irritation. He was in no mood for this today. "I do not know what you are about, *Shearsby*. How can you say things are good? And very good, at that. My wife will not even see me, let alone talk to me. What about any of this is very good?"

Shearsby grinned. "All will be well, Munsford. Trust me."

Oliver wanted to grab the man by the shoulders and shake him. "How do you know?" He dropped his hands, suddenly tired.

Shearsby placed a hand on Oliver's shoulder. "I know you have few reasons to do so, but please, trust me. All will be well and before the wager is at an end." He studied Oliver intently. "It was not an act, was it." There was no question, only a statement of fact.

Oliver shook his head. "None at all."

"I am glad to hear it." A smile hovered on Shearsby's lips and he checked his watch. "I think it best if you return home. There is nothing more you can do here." He waved a hand toward the door as he turned and walked up the stairs. Oliver was officially dismissed. He nodded to the footman as he opened the door.

He did not want to go home. It would only remind him she was not there. Perhaps he would go to Brooks's instead. Oliver shook his head as he stepped up into the carriage.

"Where to, sir?" The footman asked as he moved to shut the door.

"Home, James." Oliver would rather wallow at home than in front of those who were waiting anxiously for his marriage to fail.

He had barely one foot in the house when he felt it. Something was different in the house this morning. Oliver took several steps inside the entryway. His eyes closed and he took a deep breath. Roses. He could smell roses.

His hands went cold and his pulse pounded in his ears. Could she really be here?

He turned to Hollings. "Is Lady Munsford at home?"

Hollings nodded, but Oliver could see the twinkle in his eyes. "She is in your study, sir. I hope it acceptable. She was quite insistent."

Oliver nodded as he took the steps two at a time, shouting excitedly over his shoulder, "Not to worry, Hollings."

Oliver quickened his pace when he made it to the landing. Surely if she was in his study, she meant to stay. He fisted his hands at his side. What was he thinking? Being in his study was no guarantee of anything.

He stopped outside the door, his hand on the knob. Was he

ready for whatever was about to happen? What if she told him she did not love him? What if she wanted to withdraw to the country and live apart? He tried to swallow past the lump in his throat, but was unsuccessful.

Oliver squashed the fears. *You will not know what is to happen until you go inside.* Oh, how he wished he had some flowers in his hands, something to help hide the tremble. But he did not want to keep her waiting, lest she give up on him and leave again.

He pushed open the door and his throat squeezed so tight he could not swallow. Was it possible she had become even more beautiful? But as she drew closer, he could see she was not as well as he first assumed. Her face was pale, and her eyes slightly drawn. She looked as he felt—wrung out and tired.

"You came." The tightness in his throat made it come out as a whisper.

She nodded. Her hands were clasped behind her back and she bit her bottom lip. Oliver remembered the softness of those lips.

She took several steps toward him, her eyes never leaving his. When she was only a few steps away from him, her hands dropped to her side, one of them holding a bouquet of flowers. She thrust it forward, catching him in the chest. "These are for you."

Oliver looked down at the flowers. There was one stem each of nearly a dozen flowers and plants. Most of the flowers were red, but there were several of orange and white and purple.

"I am sorry I did not understand what you meant with the flowers." She licked her lips. "Why did you not tell me—explain to me the meaning behind them?"

Oliver shrugged. "I supposed I was afraid you would not feel the same. The flowers were a way that I could tell you how I felt, without the fear of you rejecting me."

"But if you thought I might reject you, why did you increase the wager?"

"Gah! That blasted wager." Oliver took in a stuttering breath. "When I kissed you at Fernwood—that was when I believed you truly returned my feelings." He rolled the trussed stems around between his thumb and fingers. "I am sorry I ever even made the bet. It was stupid and irresponsible."

"Why did you do it?"

Oliver took her gloveless hand in his. Her skin felt warm and soft in his hand, but he could feel her shaking. "I was at the club, the day we were married. Some of the men were speaking unkindly of you and I learned of several bets that had already been placed."

"Predicting the doom of our marriage, I suppose."

Oliver nodded. "It made me angry that these men—men who did not even know you—could be so terrible." He stared into her eyes, hoping she could see the sincerity of his words. "As misguided as it was, it was my way of stating I believed in us, in our marriage."

Rose nodded, her face softening. "Shearsby explained it might be something like that."

"I did not think how you might take it, until I heard the way Miss Carlyle made it sound." That moment would haunt his dreams for years to come.

Rose put her finger to his lips. "I find I will be most happy if we never speak her name again."

Oliver grinned beneath her finger. "I could not agree more." He sobered. "Can you ever forgive me?"

Rose pointed to the purple hyacinth. "I believe that is what this one means, does it not?"

Oliver smiled. "Have you been speaking with my mother?"

"Please, don't be angry with her."

Oliver raised a tentative hand to her face. "If she brought you back to me, I shall never be angry at her again."

Rose put her hand on top of his, leaning her head into it. "She met me at the little flower cart on St. James street and helped me choose just the right flowers to say what I needed to say."

Oliver put the flowers behind his back, "What if I wish to hear it from your lips?"

Rose pulled his hand with the flowers out from behind his back. "This was how you spoke to me, first told me how you felt about me, even if I did not understand it. Does it not stand to reason it should be the first way for me to tell you how I feel?"

He tossed the flowers on a nearby table. "I love you, Rose. And I don't want flowers to be the only way you know it."

She drew up on her tiptoes and wrapped her arms around his neck. "Oh, Oliver. I love you too. I'm sorry I ran away without allowing you to explain."

He placed a finger over her lips. "That is the past. Today we start anew."

Rose pulled her hands from around his neck and placed them on each side of his face, bringing his head down to touch hers. "Thank you for betting on me, on us. I promise that will always be a wager you will win." She raised her lips to his and the scent of roses overtook his senses.

EPILOGUE

O ne year later

ROSE STEPPED from the carriage looking up at the pale-yellow façade of Lord Trenton's London town home. Oliver squeezed her hand and tucked it gently into the crook of his arm.

Had it only been a year since she had come to London with hopes of a successful Season? She glanced at her husband and the flutter she was still not accustomed to jumped around her insides.

"Are you ready for this, my love? There is bound to be a dragon or two present, not ready to let the past fade."

Rose grinned side long at him. "I believe I still have a little fire in me yet."

Oliver leaned over and pressed a kiss to her temple. "I expected nothing less. Let's go show them what a lord deeply in love with his wife looks like."

Rose lifted a hand and placed it on his cheek. "That should not prove too difficult."

He turned his head, kissing the palm of her hand. "No, no I should say it will not."

They turned back toward the line of people entering the large house.

"Do you think we shall have the honor of seeing Miss Carlyle —or rather Mrs. Timpton? From the rumors at the club, I do not believe she can boast of the same marital felicity we have found. I heard tale the man was forced to marry her after he compromised her most cruelly. It seems the fates have given her just due," Oliver muttered.

Rose sighed softly, patting his arm. "I feel only sorrow for her. I understand how she must be feeling. I suspect she will be in need of a friend."

Oliver pulled her closer to him; putting his arm about her waist, he hugged her to his side. "Forgive me, my love. I was unkind."

He led her toward the receiving line. Rose smiled as she saw Lord Trenton smiling widely as his wife scowled just as fervently. As they approached, the man's eyes lit. "Ah, Lord Munsford. Lady Munsford. We are so pleased you accepted our invitation."

"We should not think of declining, my lord." Oliver shook the older man's hand and Rose curtsied.

She held her breath as she approached Lady Trenton, the words from last year echoing in her mind. *You brought the sister.*

"Lady Munsford." Her eyes traveled up and down Rose's front. "Your gown is quite exquisite. I should like to have the name of your modiste, if you are so inclined."

"Of course, my lady." Rose said on a breath. "Perhaps you would join me for tea."

Lady Trenton looked down her nose at Rose and gave a tight nod before looking at the next guest in line.

Rose accepted her dismissal and allowed Oliver to lead her toward a grouping of chairs where the duke and duchess were just sitting down by Lady Mayfield.

Rose leaned over, placing a kiss on her sister's cheek. "I am happy to see you arrived safely." She looked down at her sister's slightly enlarged belly. "Are you certain you feel well enough to be here tonight?"

Rose looked up at the duke's sigh.

"I tried to talk sense into her, but she insists she is well."

Violet grinned up at her husband. "I am well, Tad. I am many months from my confinement yet. I should like to get out while I am still able."

Rose sat down next to Violet. "Not to worry, Tad. I shall watch over her. I will not allow any harm to come to either of them."

Her throat tightened at the truthfulness of the statement.

One brow rose high on Violet's head. "Not you too, Rose. I had hoped you, at least, would understand." Violet put her hand over Rose's. "But I am grateful you are here, sister."

"As am I." Rose looked around them, her thoughts and feelings in such a different place than when last they were here.

Oliver pushed himself to standing and extended his hand out to her. "Before anyone is forced to leave, I intend to dance with my wife." He winked and Rose felt her face warm. "Or perhaps just show her Lord Trenton's gardens. I've heard tale they are not so very well lit."

CONTINUE READING

The next book in the series A Princess for the Gentleman on Amazon.

AFTERWORD

Dear Reader,

Thank you so much for reading The Baron's Rose. I hope you love it as much as I do.

As I was finishing writing An American in Duke's Clothing, I realized that Rose needed her own story. She was a villain that was really not so villainous, deep, deep down. I found that she was easier to write than I thought she would be, because there have been times in my life (as I am sure you've had in yours) where I felt justified in my actions toward someone due to a wrong they had inflicted upon me.

I could feel her pain and her guilt and even at times her anger. But in the end, I came to understand her and LOVE her. I hope you had a similar experience.

All of the places that were visited in this story are actually entertainments and places that people would have attended in the Regency period. The Elgin Marbles are still playing a significant role in Britain, even today. If you have a chance to look up any of

245

them, I highly recommend it. They are amazing places and give a little glimpse into the life and times of Regency London.

As for the language of flowers, as the Dowager Lady Munsford said, it has been around for a thousand years or more. There are mentions of flower symbolism dating back to the times of Plato and Aristotle. And it was, indeed, mentioned by Shakespeare in his play, Hamlet. While the symbolism of flowers did not become common knowledge until the Victorian era, it is not unimaginable that there were people during the Regency that had this knowledge.

You can checking in with me on my website Mindyburbidgestrunk

Keep up to date with my new releases by joining my newsletter here

Be sure to check out my other books:

An American in Duke's Clothing

Mistaken Identity

Miss Marleigh's Pirate Lord

Reforming the Gambler

Happy reading!

Mindy

ALSO BY MINDY BURBIDGE STRUNK

Regency House Party Series

Mistaken Identity

Miss Marleigh's Pirate Lord

Scoundrels, Rakes and Rogues Series

Reforming the Gambler

Rake on the Run

The Secrets of a Scoundrel

Unlikely Match Series

An American in Dukes Clothing

The Baron's Rose

A Princess for the Gentleman

Bells of Christmas Series

Unmasking Lady Caroline

Thawing the Viscount's Heart

The Son's of Somerset Series

The Stable Master's Son

Hidden Riches Series

The Mysteries of Hawthorn Hall

Top Flight Series

Bear: A Fighter Pilot Romance

Mustang: A Fighter Pilot Romance

ABOUT THE AUTHOR

Mindy loves all things history and romance, which makes reading and writing Regency romance right up her alley. Since she was a little girl, playing in her imaginary closet elevator, she has always had stories running through her mind. But it wasn't until she was well into adulthood, that she realized she could write those stories down. Now they occupy her dreams and most every quiet moment that she has-she often washes her hair two or three times because she can't remember doing it the first time. This usually means really clean hair and hopefully a fixed plot hole. When she isn't living in her alternate realities, she is married to her real-life Mr. Darcy and trying to raise five proper boys (two of which are twins!). They live happily in the beautiful mountains of Utah.

Printed in Great Britain
by Amazon

17104439R00145